Bucked

Blue Collar Bad Boys, Volume 8

Brill Harper

Published by Brill Harper, 2018.

BUCKED

First edition. January 17, 2018.

Copyright © 2018 Brill Harper.

ISBN: 979-8223779742

Written by Brill Harper.

About this Book

S *ave a horse...*

Ruby Grant is dead-broke when she wins an all-inclusive vacation to Paradise Hotel in Wyoming. She can't wait to sip expensive champagne while lounging in a bathtub full of bubbles. To her horror, she discovers "Paradise" is actually *Pair-A-Dice* Ranch and nothing like the brochure. She's ready to hop on the next plane back to LA, but sexy cowboy Dusty Cassidy offers her an irresistible deal if she'll stay. This may not be the vacation she envisioned, but Dusty is just the man for her needs—whether he knows it or not, he's going to be her first lover.

Ride a cowboy...

Dusty can't decide if Ruby is an angel in white the daughter of the devil. Her curves are so dangerously sexy they should be outlawed. All his time and energy belongs to the ranch, so he definitely doesn't need a pretty little city girl tempting him away from his chores. Fortunately, she'll only be on the ranch for a week, so he won't have to worry about any expectations. But when her vacation comes to an end, will he be able to let her go?

Author's confession: Yeehaw! You know by now that I love my tropes. If you love cowboys, Dusty is going to steal your freaking heart faster than he steals Ruby's virginity. If you're tired of billionaires and want a real man hero, this book is for you. It doesn't hurt that, like all my bad boy heroes, he's really a gooey alphamallow on the inside. (If you're one of my "safe read" lovers, you can rest easy. No other woman drama here.)

Chapter One

Ruby

The last time I was in a limousine was prom night in Ohio when I was seventeen years old. That was six years ago. A year later, I moved to Los Angeles, thinking that my life would be limos and champagne and handsome movie stars every day.

As you can probably guess, that's not how things worked out.

At all.

My glamorous life includes working behind the front desk of a three-star chain hotel, eating questionable takeout because it's *probably* not moldy yet and payday is still two days away, and acting in an occasional commercial for orange juice or zit cream.

My Oscar speech is ready, though. I've been working on it since I was twelve.

Truth be told, I was getting close to calling my folks for bus fare back home when I got the message that I won an all-expense paid trip to Paradise Ranch. I'm a city girl, but I wasn't going to turn it down. It felt like a lifeline when I needed it most. Massages, gourmet food, 1,000-count sheets, and drinking poolside. Maybe the cabana boys wear Stetsons. A girl can only hope.

Finally, the universe was taking pity on me.

I settle back into my plush limo seat and pretend this is what my life is like every day. What would it feel like to not worry all the time? To have the satisfaction of knowing your bills are paid and you can still eat without visiting the food bank every couple of months. To be able to buy a new outfit once in a while and not have to skip a payment on your light bill because of it? To not have to choose between your dignity and your survival?

I used to want the mansions and the pools and the fancy cars. Now I just want to not be worried all the time and maybe even enjoy the work I'm doing. They aren't big goals really. It shouldn't seem out of the realm of possibility that I don't have to choose between buying a loaf of bread or having enough quarters for the dryer.

We've been driving quite a while and the champagne is starting to take its toll on my bladder. But the driver assures me we are almost there.

Imagine. Me in paradise. Finally, finally, finally things are going my way. It might only be for a week, but I am going to enjoy the hell out of it. I think about the red lacy lingerie I packed. I've had the bra and panties for a year and a half and haven't worn them once. I've been saving them for a special occasion, and well, I haven't had any special occasions in twice as long as that.

In my fantasies, I put them on for a third date with a fabulous CEO who's been wooing me with wine and roses. I'd wear them under a pretty little black dress that makes his eyes goggle whenever he looks at me. After a four-course meal and dancing, we'd go back to his place and I'd reveal my lacy secrets after he declares his love. We'd make love, and I'd be glad I waited until this night. My patience would be rewarded, and the sex would be glorious.

So far, though, third dates have been scarce. When I put the lingerie in my suitcase, I decided that this vacation was the perfect time to have a fling. I deserve to have a great memory of losing my virginity. Since I haven't found the guy who wines and dines me and professes his love, then maybe it's time I look for someone else. A vacation fling. Someone impossibly hot. Someone whose memory gives me that secret smile whenever I remember my week in paradise years from now.

So this week is about rest, rejuvenation, and revving my motor without powering up my vibrator.

We really have been driving for a long time. It's pretty remote, but rich people like that kind of thing maybe. The endless pastures and fields are starting to make me edgy, but I pretend I'm rich and I love it, unwrapping one of those fancy hazelnut candies that I don't really care for but make me feel like I'm living large.

We slow and make a turn, finally, onto a long, dirt road. Horses are galloping through the pasture on my right, but as we slow, I see chickens chasing each other around a tractor.

A tractor at a spa?

This can't be right.

I tap on the glass that separates me from the car driver. "Excuse me, Mr. Nichols?" He doesn't open the window, but pushes the intercom I had forgotten about.

"Yes, Ms. Grant?"

"I think we made a wrong turn. We're supposed to be going to Paradise Ranch."

"Yes, Ms. Grant." He points to a painted sign near a ranch house. "Pair-a-Dice Ranch. We're here."

He stops the car and my hopes are just...decimated. Once again, the universe has turned my own dreams on me. The sign clearly says Pair-a-Dice.

I should have known. Why hadn't I prepared to be let down? That's what always happens to me. If I didn't have bad luck, I'd have no luck at all.

What was I really expecting, though? Of course filling out a contest entry at a discount grocery store wasn't going to net me a four-star vacation. Of course it was a scam. Now what? Do I want to make the best of it or should I even bother getting out of this car? I look around. It's pretty outside with trees in the distance...and the house looks nice—but it's clearly a dusty working ranch and not going to be what I wanted.

I'm going to call this one more of life's hard lessons and go home. I might still be able to get put on the schedule at work. I never should have taken the time off anyway. I have vacation time on the books, but I'm allowed to work through it and take the pay. I need the pay.

I needed the time off too, but that's just not how my life goes.

That's when I see him.

He's...well...huge. I suppose that it could be the angle or the perspective of the distance to the front porch he's standing on, but he looks like a giant wearing tight blue jeans and a white tank top. And a hat and cowboy boots, of course. I live in LA, so it's not like I don't see a lot of men walking around shirtless with good bodies. But he is stunning.

My mouth goes dry and my skin tingles. He's some kind of beast man. Larger than life surely. His shirt is molded to muscles earned by hard work and battling nature, not weight machines and running on a track that goes nowhere. He starts off the porch, his swagger not exaggerated, but it's there. His beefy legs are encased in denim that must struggle to keep the seams together.

Everything about him is brutally beautiful, his face no exception. He is the opposite of the man in my fantasies, the one who wears suits and power so well. This guy, he wears the sun. He's bronzed everywhere and when he gets close enough to the car to talk to Mr. Nichols, I see he even has creases near his eyes, probably from looking at the sky.

I can't hear what they are saying, so I open my own door and walk around the car.

Shit, he's even bigger than I imagined. He towers over me, but he's got this masculine grace that makes me feel instantly safe. That's crazy and I've lived in the city long enough to know that. But I feel it all the same.

"Hey, darlin', welcome to Pair-a-Dice ranch. I'm the owner, Dusty Cassidy. Mr. Nichols here tells me you've been given a bit of a shock. I reckon a glass of sweet tea and some conversation is in order."

I reckon if I drink one more thing before I use a bathroom I'll be in bad shape. I can't make it all the way back to the airport without a pit stop.

He reaches his big paw out to me, and I gingerly offer him my much smaller hand. He's got cowboy hands—rough and callused. I get a tickle in my spine thinking about how the texture would feel against the skin under my clothes.

Wait, no. Stop that. *He is not for you.* This is not happening.

"What's your name, darlin'?"

I blink. I'm not saying I forgot my name, but I think I forgot my name.

Mr. Nichols steps up. "This is Ruby Grant. Ms. Grant, I'm sure you'd like to freshen up. I'll wait here at the car until you decide if you want to stay."

Once again, I'm feeling a sense of safety that I shouldn't. But Mr. Nichols reminds me of my own dad. It's clear he's not going to just drop me here unless I want to be left.

Could I stay? It's not what I planned, but it's still a week out of LA madness.

A woman steps out onto the porch, her silver hair pulled back from her face. "Get that girl out of the sun, Chuck."

"Yes, dear," Mr. Nichols answers. "That's my wife. She'll show you to the ladies' room. She does the cooking here."

I eye the porch. I'm either stepping into some sort of elaborate kidnapping plot, or these are warm, nice people. Either way, I need to use the bathroom, and I'd rather face the danger with an empty bladder.

Dusty

THE LITTLE FILLY THE universe just dropped into my world is the sexiest thing I ever laid eyes on. I wait until she's already in the house when I turn to her driver.

"Uncle Chuck, what have you done?" Besides renting a limousine.

"You said you needed more bookings and to get more bookings, you needed more of those internet things."

"Reviews?"

"Yeah."

"That girl did not come prepared to spend a vacation at a dude ranch. She's got city girl written all over her."

"We might have spruced up the place in the ad."

He's my uncle. I love him. Right now, I'd like to kill him. "You want to get my license taken away for false advertising?"

"It's not like she paid money for something she isn't going to get. It's a free trip. All-expenses paid. All she had to do was promise to leave a review."

"And you think she's going to leave a good review after she finds out she's basically been kidnapped and dumped here when she was expecting something else?"

"That's where you come in. You just need to show her a good time. Make sure she falls in love with Pair-a-Dice. She's a city girl—nobody needs this place more than those city people.

"City people live in the city for a reason, old man. They like it."

Uncle Chuck shrugs. "They don't know any better."

It's impossible to stay mad at my uncle for long. He's got nothing but the best intentions, even if the meddling he and Aunt Charlotte do can get tiresome.

I pinch the bridge of my nose. I don't need this complication right now. It's hard enough renovating this place for a future tourist attraction while keeping the un-tourist parts working. "What was she expecting? What did you offer in the ad?"

"It wasn't an ad. It was a contest."

I'm not even going to go into detail with him about all the laws he probably broke with his contest or lottery or raffle. I'm sure she wasn't a random winner, either. They probably handpicked her out of whatever entries they got. Likely they have ulterior motives. They've been too quiet about my bachelor status lately, and it should have sent up a bunch of red flags. I was just so relieved that they'd seemed to let it go and the matchmaking attempts had slowed down. I should have known better. "What does she think she won?"

"A week at Pair-a-Dice Ranch."

"What aren't you telling me?"

"We spelled it Paradise. You know...i-s-e."

The muscles in my jaw constrict into a tight band. "And what does Paradise have to offer a city girl like her?"

He throws his chauffeur hat into to the limo, exposing his bald head. "Relaxation. Nature walks. Horseback riding..."

All things we currently have. "What aren't you telling me?"

"Gourmet meals. Spa. Massages."

Things we don't have but are in the plan for someday.

"Maybe a pool."

"A pool?" Jesus, Mary, and Joseph. A pool. That's not even in the five-year plan.

"You can just tell her it's out of commission. The river is more refreshing anyway. And Charlotte's cooking is better than gourmet, you know that."

As if a woman ready for an infinity pool would rather dunk herself in a river. "And the massages? What's your plan there?"

"We borrowed a table from that place in town for the week."

"Did you happen to borrow a massage therapist to go with it?"

He looks sheepish, but I ain't fooled. My family has given me plenty of grief over getting my massage therapy license while in college. At the time, I signed up because the instructor was hot. Turns out I liked it well enough to stick with it to get a certificate while I was working on my business degree. It's a good skill to have, but I took a lot of good-natured teasing over the years.

Until now of course. When they want me to grope the California hothouse flower.

"That girl in there has every right to go to the police with this scam. What you and Charlotte pulled could get us into a lot of trouble."

"We just wanted to help you. She's a nice girl. She won't get mad."

"Get mad? Uncle Chuck, you brought her here under false pretenses. She probably took time off work to come. She's going to be spitting mad and I can't blame her."

"Then show her what's great about Pair-a-Dice. She'll have a wonderful time and then you'll get the review you want so much."

Like one review is going to change everything. My aunt and uncle really don't understand the internet at all. My only hope is that one more bad review won't sink me. The previous owners really ran the place into the ground. I have grand plans for this ranch, but I need to keep an income coming in to fund the improvements. Right now, my clientele includes hikers, fishermen, and a few horseback riding enthusiasts.

Not one of them is looking for four-star accommodations. Some of them don't even want a working shower.

"Get her to stay, son. That's the hard part. Once she's here, she'll love it."

I'm trying to stay patient. Really I am. My aunt and uncle helped my father raise me after my mom died. And when he died a few years back, no one was more surprised than me that I had an inheritance. Not a big one, but big enough to buy my own land. My family's been very supportive of my vision and dug right in on day one to help me. But I still get frustrated from time to time. "The ends don't justify the means."

"Don't pull out your fancy college words now."

I roll my eyes at him. "You know very well what that means, and I didn't learn that in college. Stop trying to distract me from the real issue here."

The front door opens, and my aunt comes out holding a tray of sweet tea, Ms. Ruby Grant shyly following.

That girl does something to me. I don't know how to explain it. I've never been hit so hard with want just from seeing a woman. She up and grassed me like a greenhorn. She's not movie star pretty, which is not something I like anyway. No, she's got an interesting face and a short, curvy body. I want to squeeze those sweet curves. Damn. If I don't change my line of thinking, everyone is going to see the evidence of it in my pants.

Real class act, Dusty.

I don't want to scare the girl. And I've already got six feet and four inches going against me. I know I'm a big man. Intimidating to some. Especially women. I'd like to say I'm a gentle giant, but there's been a time or two when I've had to use what God me gave to protect what's mine or fend off a bully or two from someone less able to defend themselves. I don't have any problems using my fists or my strength to set things right when necessary, but it's never my first choice.

Lord knows my size is imposing, though.

We join the ladies on the porch. Ruby is like a little nervous rabbit, and I feel like a giant wolf taking the chair next to her at the tiny table. Ready to eat her whole maybe. My heart ratchets up. What is wrong with me? Sure, I've been too busy for dating for a bit, but my reaction to this young woman is off the charts for me.

We all drink our tea in awkward silence. Shit. I bet the city boys she is used to could fill the silence much better. But what can I say? *Would you care to tour our spa facilities?* The ones we don't have?

"So, Ms. Grant," Uncle Chuck begins.

"Please call me Ruby," she answers. "All of you." She sends a sly sideways glance in my direction, and her cheeks pinken.

Fuck me, but I love that look on her. Sweet and shy, yet I know underneath she's got sass. I'm damn near punched in the gut with desire for this woman and we've hardly spoken.

Uncle Chuck begins again, "Ruby, it seems the contest you entered began prematurely. As you can see, Pair-a-Dice isn't quite ready for all the things they plan to offer."

She sends my uncle a bland look. "Also, it wasn't proofread very well. Pair-a-Dice...Paradise."

I cough.

"Dusty can give you a tour of things. There's river rafting, horseback riding, and miles of trails for hiking."

Ruby does not look convinced that this is her ideal vacation. I don't blame her. But something in me is almost desperate to find a way to make her stay. Which means I should let this lie. We'd both be better off if she went on home and pretended none of this happened. I'm in no position to court her—I have to get this ranch on its feet. And she doesn't seem the quick tumble type.

But hell.

"What have you got to lose, Ruby? If you don't want to stay, Chuck here will drive you back to the airport."

She gets this pensive look on her face, and I add one more emotion to my catalog of her expressions. I don't know what kind of pretty little witch she is, but I have never felt like this before.

Ruby takes a long sip of tea. "All right. Show me around."

My jeans tighten as my dick searches for hidden meaning in her words. I'd love to show her lots of things. I'm more interested in what she might show me, though.

If things were different, of course.

Pair-a-Dice has seen better days, I suppose. But no one can argue that God didn't pay special attention to my land. I take Ruby to the places that I haven't had to do much to first. The woods behind the house leading to the river never fail to ease my stress. I don't suppose it's the same for her, but I don't know what a girl who likes Los Angeles might like. A sandy beach? A concrete pool? I truly don't know. But she only hesitates for a second about entering the woods with me, and I feel like an idiot for not realizing that she might not feel safe.

Little Ruby Riding Hood and the Big, Bad Wolf

"I know you don't know me, Ruby. And I know I look more like a mountain than a man, but I promise you're safe with me. I would never let anyone or anything bad happen to you. Myself included."

She huffs out a laugh. "If you knew the kinds of men who say that exact same things to girls in LA, you would realize how not reassuring that is."

I stop walking. I'm angry that maybe someone hurt her. I'm upset that she doesn't trust me. I'm embarrassed that I'm acting like such a fool. All these things hit me at once. "I'm sorry. Why don't we just go back to the house? I don't want to make you uncomfortable."

I turn on the trail, but she stops me, her tiny hand on my arm. "No, it's okay. Please. I want to see the river. I trust you."

My heart damn near breaks out of my ribcage. She trusts me. I can't explain why that means so much to me.

Whoa there, Hoss.

Shit. This woman is trouble.

I learned my lesson about city girls the hard way, and I don't intend to make the same mistake twice.

I can enjoy her company. But that's it. I don't need to let her mess with my emotions.

"So, tell me what is really going on with this ranch," she says after we walk a bit. "Some things aren't really adding up for me."

My fool heart is telling me to make something up. Keep her here any way I can. But that wouldn't be right. And she trusts me. I'm a man of honor, no matter how hard the zipper of my pants is pressing into my growing cock. "My aunt and uncle mean well."

"Mr. Nichols is your uncle, then?"

I nod. She's got city smarts, no sense lying to her. I get the feeling she's been lied to enough. "They're trying to help me rebuild the ranch. They heard me talking about the bad reviews and got it in their heads to bring me a guest, I suppose."

"Why do you need reviews?"

"I haven't owned Pair-a-Dice long. I got it for a song—but that was before I realized the damn record was broken. There's a lot of good here, but the previous owners let it fall into disrepair. They were also not so good at hospitality. I'm trying to fix everything and learn what I need to know about managing a resort, but we aren't ready for guests. Not the resort kind. I've got the cabins set up still for campers, but my vision of Pair-a-Dice is a long ways off."

She bites her lip. "I see...the pool?"

"There is no pool."

"The full-service spa?"

"Yeah, none of that either. Yet. It's actually not a bad idea."

Her resigned expression is one I never want to see again. Like she's used to disappointment. "Massages are out then."

What the hell. "I will personally give you a massage every day. There's a table at the house." Somewhere.

"Right." She pulls in her shoulders, trying to make herself smaller.

Idiot bastard. Now you've gone and got her hackles up.

"Not like that," I blurt out. "I'm actually a licensed massage therapist. It's all on the up-and-up."

"You're a licensed massage therapist cowboy?"

Ouch. Her incredulous expression isn't doing much for my ego either.

"I can show you the paperwork."

"You have paperwork?"

"Yes, ma'am. State licensing board agrees that I am a verifiable and legitimately licensed therapist."

We've returned to the back porch now and she stops, showing me a new emotion as her eyes twinkle with amusement. "Well, this trip just got interesting."

She's a good sport and I really like this girl. "I know you signed up for a different kind of vacation. But I promise you, if you stay, you won't regret it."

God, she smells good, too. It's a sweet scent. A little like cotton candy.

"All right, cowboy. I expect to be pampered if I'm leaving this review you need so much."

We both know that one positive review isn't going to change the tide, but she's got this wry smile and a secret behind her eyes and I'm going to find out what that's all about if it's the last thing I do.

Chapter Two

Ruby

Mrs. Nichols shows me to my room in the main house after my walk with Dusty. There are secluded cabins not too far away, but I don't feel like being isolated at night. Not when I overheard one of the ranch hands tell Dusty they lost another chicken to a coyote last night. I'm not sure if coyotes are dangerous to humans or not, but I'm not up for finding out the hard way.

Of course, I didn't take danger too seriously when I agreed to stay.

Not when they told me cell service is spotty to none.

Not when they told me there was no Wi-Fi.

Not when they told me town was thirteen miles away.

Not when I saw the bulge in my cowboy host's Wrangler jeans.

I'm not going to think about that too much right now. If that means I'm burying my head in the sand, so be it.

"Here's your room, missy. I expect you'll like it just fine." Charlotte gestures me in, and I'm taken aback.

It's more than lovely. A huge bed dominates the room with yards and yards of a white duvet puffed up with down. It's starkly bright against the gleaming dark pillars of the four posts around it. The floor shines between braided rugs and smells like lemon.

"Mrs. Nichols, it's gorgeous."

She smiles, her crooked tooth endears and charms me. "I expect the minute I close this door, you'll be jumping on the bed. It's as tempting as a pile of leaves to a child."

"You read my mind."

My bags are already on a bench, ready for me to unpack. There's an overstuffed chair in the corner with an inviting throw for a perfect reading nook. Which is good since there's no television or even a phone in the room.

"Are all the rooms like this? So beautiful?"

"They're all pretty, but this one is the biggest and best. The main house is finished. The team is working on building the chuck house and saloon now. Dusty has some big ideas. He's a good man. A strong man."

I catch her gaze as she watches me. I have a feeling she's not talking about his brute strength, since that's obvious in the way he's built like an ox. "He doesn't seem afraid of a little hard work. This place is going to need a lot of elbow grease to be as grand as ...say...the advertisement I saw for the contest."

She narrows her eyes and chuffs at me, not the least bit ashamed of what she did. "The grand part of his plan is already here. The forest, the horses, the river, the sky. You won't ever see anywhere else like it. The buildings and massages and gourmet stuff, that's just icing on the cake. You'll see. You'll fall in love with Pair-a-Dice. We all did."

She leaves me to unpack, and I fumble when I get to the red lingerie. I can't help but think of Dusty and what his hands would look like as he peels the lace from my body. Would he be the gentleman cowboy? All pleases and ma'ams. Or would he be more like a wolf, tearing and snapping and feral?

My face heats up just thinking about the possibilities.

I could use some of that sweet tea right about now. I finish unpacking and grab my Kindle. There's a lovely porch swing in the shade I want to try. Maybe this won't be so bad.

I stop in the kitchen and ask for some tea, but Charlotte insists she'll bring it out. I'm a guest, after all. I hate bothering her, but I know they want to impress me, so I should be gracious and make sure I seem suitably impressed. That would be the nice thing to do.

I'm about five minutes into my book when the sun is blocked by Paul Bunyan in a tuxedo. What in the world?

"Dusty? Is that you?"

"Miss Ruby, Charlotte says you ordered tea."

He's trying so hard to be formal as he lays out my tea and cute little crustless sandwiches that I giggle. When his face gets all red, I feel like a shit. "I'm sorry, Dusty. It's just. I'm not sure what is happening right now. Why are you wearing a tuxedo in the middle of the afternoon and serving me iced tea?"

"Uncle Chuck rented the monkey suit." He yanks off the clip-on tie. "I guess he thought it would make the resort part more believable."

Everyone is trying so earnestly to make me have a nice time. The best room, the limo, the tuxedo-wearing cowboy. It's all very sweet, if not a tad silly. "Can I tell you something without it coming off like criticism? As someone who's worked in the hotel business for five years?"

A lot of men bristle when a woman tries to give them advice, but Dusty gets this really open look on his face, like he's ready to soak up any knowledge I can impart. "I didn't know you worked in a hotel. I'd love advice."

"Well, it's just a chain hotel. Nothing fancy. But I know a thing or two about guests. You want to give them the experience they paid for or expect. This is a ranch. Your guests don't want tuxedos. They want cowboys and horses and to feel like they're part of the experience. Even if it's wrapped up in luxury."

"So, you don't think I should have waitstaff in formal attire?" He grins, and I realize he doesn't either. He's wearing the tuxedo because his uncle got it for him, and he would rather please his uncle than shame him. "How about chaps? Maybe next time, I should serve you wearing chaps."

The thought of Dusty wearing chaps...and nothing else...pops into my mind. Judging from the smile on his face, that was his intention. You could sizzle bacon on my cheeks right now.

Dusty Cassidy is way out of my league. I've never dated anyone as hot or manly or driven. He's got the kind of confidence that tells a girl he knows his way around a woman's body. And I think he's flirting with me.

I could flirt back. I want to. But it would be so humiliating to be brushed off. Then I'd spend the week avoiding him and hiding in my room. Which would be a shame because I think he's nice and interesting, on top of being a total hottie, and I'd miss out on his company. I'm too nervous to make many guy friends where I live. The ones I come into contact with are either trying to move up the ladder and don't care who they push out of the way to get to the next rung, or they have no ambition at all and don't care who they have to be nice to if they can couch surf at your place.

Dusty is different from any man I've ever talked to. He's attentive, and open-minded, and a true gentleman. He's also ambitious, but in the good way. He wants to build something great. He wants to please his family. He seems so at ease in nature.

I just...I really want to get to know him. I don't want to lose the connection I feel by trying too hard and lobbing a flirtation at him that misses the mark.

But if I don't try, I'll never know. And isn't that worse?

Hell, I'm never going to see him again after this week. I might as well have a little fun. If nothing else, I can practice flirting so I can improve my range when I get back home. And if things go really well, my cowboy can teach me how to ride a stallion.

Easy, girl.

Here goes nothing.

"So Dusty, how does a guest go about booking her massage?"

Dusty

AFTER DINNER, AFTER my aunt and uncle retire to their own cabin, I set up the massage table in Ruby's room. This is probably a mistake. I should not be touching a guest. Yeah, I'm a professional, but I don't have professional feelings toward Ms. Ruby Grant, and I'm not sure if I'm going to be able to convince either of us otherwise.

At the very least, I should have set up the massage in an empty guest room. But I wanted her to be able to relax right away in the room and bathroom she's already settled in.

I can do this. I might be horny as fuck, but I'm a man, not an animal.

Most of the time.

I set up the tray with the oils and turn on the soft spa music. The quiet snick of the bathroom door lets me know she's come out. I take a deep breath and turn.

Fuck me, she's beautiful.

She's got her face clean of makeup and her hair in some messy kind of bun, and she's wrapped in one of the soft white robes we ordered for the guests. She shouldn't be so striking, but I feel like a dagger of lightning just wracked my body and the jolts are still zapping in my pants.

"Are you ready?" I ask, praying she'll change her mind and hoping to God she won't. I want to get my hands on that milky skin. I'm itching to glide my fingers around her curves. She's got so many sweet ones.

She nods nervously. "I've only had one other massage before. It was...not like this."

Her nerves steady mine. I feel useful when I can soothe her. "If anything makes you uncomfortable, you just let me know. The object here is for you to relax."

"Right." She nods briskly in the direction of the table. "I'll just go get on that then."

"There's a towel you can wrap around yourself loosely. I can move it as I get to other parts of your body." I turn for her privacy. "Lie on your stomach and let me know when you're ready."

The sound of her robe hitting the bed sends me a mental picture I'd give anything to see in real time. I wonder if she left her panties on—I gave her the option to wear them or not, whichever made her more comfortable. "I'm ready."

I take another deep breath and turn back to her. Holy shit. This is torture and bliss at the same time. She's laid out like she's on an all-you-can-eat buffet table. And I'm a man with a hearty appetite.

She shivers, trembling softly. "Are you cold, sweetness?"

"A little."

I pour some oil into my hands and rub my palms together. "The oil is warm. We'll get you comfortable in no time. I'm just going to drizzle a bit on your back, okay?"

"Okay."

I start with her shoulders, using my palms to work in the lavender oil and loosen the tense muscles around her neck. It's been a while since I've given a massage, but I find a rhythm that gently works her back and shoulders like waves lapping against the shore. I like this communion with another person. I like feeling the tension leave her body.

I wouldn't want to do it all the time, but I sure as hell want to keep going.

She's breathing deeper now. More relaxed. My hands are slowly working around her ribcage, closer and closer to her naked breasts, my fingers caressing the soft flesh on the sides.

This is dangerously close to crossing the line, but my cock is so hard I'm ready to explode. Her body is soft and sweet. She's got just the right amount of cushion for a man. I want to roll her over and show her how long and hard this cowboy can ride.

"Tell me about the ranch. Wait...is it okay to talk?"

"That's completely up to you. Most people prefer a little small talk, but remain mostly quiet. Some people don't talk at all. Some yak a fella's ear off."

"I hate small talk." She sighs. "But I am really interested in your plans. Charlotte says you're working on the chuck house and saloon right now."

This is good. Talking. It's helping me stay distracted from the things I really want to do to her body.

"Yeah, eventually, I want to be able to have about fifty guests at a time. We'll serve three squares in the chuck house, and have events like dances in the saloon. Those cabins will all be outfitted with fireplaces and quality amenities. And we have ten rooms here in the main house."

I get to a decent-sized knot in her back and work it with more pressure until she groans happily. "That feels better already. So where does all the horseback riding take place?"

"We ride in the surrounding Buckhorn National Forest. It's pretty spectacular. You ride?"

"Horses? No."

My hand stills. Fuck. So much for distracting me away from thoughts of sex.

"I used to ride quads with my dad and brothers in Ohio."

Right. Quads. "Ohio is where you grew up?"

"Yeah. I lived there until I moved to Los Angeles."

Eventually I start moving down, stopping every now and then to readjust the towel so that it covers less and less of her body.

"That feels really good. What you're doing." She moans again, and I feel the precum leaking from my dick. I want to hear that sound again, only I want to be balls-deep in her when she makes it.

"You have magic hands, Dusty."

I squeeze my eyes shut and try to think of anything at all to distract me from the feel of her flesh under my hands. The sound of her pleasure. The scent of her mixed with the oil.

Does she know how much I want her? Does she want me back? Is that what this is? Her request for a massage. The comments. Or is she innocent? Just telling me I'm doing a good job. Just trying to make the best of her vacation gone awry.

I'm probably going to die of blue balls, but the right thing to do is stay professional.

"Tell me more about yourself, Ruby." Maybe she's a horrible person, and the more I get to know her, her terrible qualities will shine through. Maybe then I'll forget all about her silky skin and tender thighs.

"There's not much to tell. I'm not like you, working hard on my dream." She pauses. "Sometimes, I feel like I don't even have a dream anymore."

My hands still on her skin. "What's your dream, sweetheart?"

"I used to want to be a famous actress. But I've been in LA for a long time, and other than a few commercials, I'm just...surviving, I guess. I can't even say I'm still trying, really."

I resume my massage, determined to help her feel better. "Maybe your dream has changed. There's nothing wrong with that. I went away to college to get away from ranching, and look where I ended back up."

"LA sort of takes it out of you. I just sort of...stopped wishing."

"That's the saddest thing I've heard, Ruby. You just need to find your next wish is all. Maybe a week here in the mountains will help."

"Maybe."

She starts shifting, so I pull my hands back so she can get comfortable, only she rolls all the way onto her back.

"Is it time to do my front?"

Chapter Three

Ruby

The shocked look on Dusty's face melts into pure lust.

I'm being brazen as hell. But I need a new wish, like he said, and my new wish is to not sit on the sidelines of my life and wonder what it feels like to really live. I wish to know what it feels like to give myself to a man

To have an honest-to-God orgasm in the company of another person.

He's staring at my breasts now. But still not touching me. The heat of my blush starts on my cheeks but radiates out. My scalp, my chest, it's all on fire. Did I get it wrong? Is this not what he wanted too?

Why am I so stupid? I'm as vulnerable as a person can get right now, half naked laying on a table in front of a full clothed man. He could do anything he wants to me, and he's not interested.

This cannot be happening. Am I really that clueless?

If I were any kind of actress at all, I would get into character, any character, and save face. Pretend I'm not me. That his rejection doesn't burn like cold fire.

But, truthfully, I don't think I can act my way out of a paper bag. That's part of my problem in Hollywood. I loved being on stage in my high school plays, but being a working actress is a lot different. I've just been too stubborn to call it quits.

I won't make that mistake right now. I'm reaching for the towel to cover up when he finally speaks. "Are you sure about this? This is what you want?"

I yank up the towel. "I don't want to force you to do something you don't want to do, cowboy."

As for me, I'm moving back to Ohio. I'll get a job just like the one I have in hopefully a better neighborhood and get seven cats and eat whatever I want and just... screw my dreams. To hell with them. They never got me very far.

And screw men, for that matter. Or...the opposite of screw men.

I have batteries. I don't need a fantasy man. I don't need racy red lingerie that's probably uncomfortable to wear anyway. I don't need to know what it's like to be filled up with someone else. To lose myself to sensation. I'll be just fine on my own.

Who needs a husband or kids even? My brothers will settle down soon, and I can be an awesome auntie. I don't need anything else. I'm not going to shed one more tear over being passed over again and again.

I need to come to terms with the fact that something about me just isn't good enough. Not for acting. Not for dating. Not even for a quick, no-strings, you don't even have to work for it I'm already naked on a flat surface fling.

"Darlin', there's very little I don't want to do to you right now."

I roll my eyes and sit up, the blood rushing from my head. "Yeah, you seem like a man at the end of his tether right now. You're barely refraining, I can tell." I glance over and get a peek of the bulge in his track pants. He's either really hard or he's storing a hammer in there. "Oh."

"Yeah, 'oh.' The problem isn't that I'm not at the end of my tether. I'm there. Believe me. I'm trying to be a gentleman."

It's too late. I am not setting myself up for more rejection. Not anymore.

One more try.

No.

C'mon, girl. One more, and if it doesn't work out, you never have to try again.

No. He doesn't want me.

It looks like he wants you. What do you have to lose?

Nothing. I have absolutely nothing left to lose. One last shred of dignity isn't doing me any good. He'd be a generous lover. He's the hottest man I've ever been alone with.

Maybe I'm not worth one more try. But he is.

While I'm having this crazy internal argument with myself, that bulge keeps getting impossibly bigger. I draw on the memory of what it was like when I used to get on the stage in high school. Back when I thought, hell, everyone thought, I was a good actress. Back when I believed in myself. My talent. My worth. The big fish who didn't know she was swimming in a very small pond. That girl still has to be inside me somewhere, right? And it's time to make her a woman.

One more try.

I stare at his pants another second more and bite my lip as I raise my eyes slowly up the rest of his granite hard body until they meet with his. His nostrils flare slightly and his eyes get darker.

Lights. Camera. Action.

"Then I must not be doing this seduction thing right." *Which is no surprise.* "I was hoping that maybe I had what it takes to bring out the very bad cowboy that I'm sure you're hiding in there."

He's grinding his jaw so hard, his mandible is ticking. "Be careful what you wish for, Ruby," he tells me through clenched teeth.

"That's just it. I'm done wishing, Dusty. I'm ready for action, not daydreams. I promised myself a fling on this trip, and if you're not interested, maybe I'll just keep looking."

Liar.

Shush. Keep it up.

His eyes narrowed. "Keep looking?"

I shrug with exaggeration. "You have a nice construction crew working with you. About six men to choose from. Plus the wranglers. You're my first choice, but—"

His hand over my mouth stops my train of thought. "Don't finish that sentence, little girl. I'm a man on the edge as it is. Nobody else touches you. You understand?"

The flutter in my stomach understands. Growly, jealous cowboys are delicious.

I nod and he removes his hand. "What's it going to take to push you *over* the edge then, cowboy?"

His whole body is tense, his muscles flexing under that T-shirt. So much strength and power coiled up in those beefy arms. I want to feel it. I want him wrapped around me. Trapping me. Caging me.

He closes his eyes, letting out a resigned sigh. "Lay down, Ruby. Let's finish this massage."

Not exactly what I was hoping for. What's a girl gotta do to get a ravishing around here? But I do as he says, and he yanks the towel from my body in an economy of movement that startles me.

"Relax, baby girl." His voice is lower now. Gravelly. It jumbles my insides like rocks in a tumbler. He drizzles warm oil on my chest; it trickles little rivulets over my skin. "Are you ready for more, angel?"

God, yes. "Please."

Once again, he starts on my shoulders, working the oil into my skin with his firm hands. They glide down my arms, and he picks up my wrists and ease them above my head. "Hold on to this pillow," he orders, and I do, knowing my boobs are lifting up to him wantonly. "Good girl. I bet you don't always do what you're told, do you?"

I snort.

"I don't mind a little sass. I like a challenge, city girl." His hands roam down my sides, catching some side boob, but ignoring my hard nipples. I can feel them poking the air, so needy for attention. "I'm a little worried about not being professional here. You being a guest at my resort and a client on my massage table, and all. I don't want any trouble, so we're going to make sure that everything I do to you is something you're begging for. How's that sound?"

The noise that comes out of me is a new one. A half-whimper, half-groan. This is nothing like my fantasies of a big city CEO taking my virginity politely. This is carnal, what he's making me feel. I always thought sex would be like vulnerable pieces being plucked out of me one at a time by gentle, suave hands. Instead, it feels like he wants me to just filet myself open for him. No hiding behind shy sensibilities. He's not taking anything, he's making me give myself to him.

His large hands rest just underneath my breasts. "Ask me to touch your tits, if that's what you want."

"Please."

He circles around them with those talented fingers, but doesn't touch the aching centers. "I'm going to need a little more than that."

I groan. "Please, touch my tits, Dusty."

"Good girl."

I'm rewarded with firm strokes as he cups and squeezes me. My hips start moving, desperate for more. His hands cup my breasts and he drags his fingernails in circles around my nipples, making sure not to touch. I moan and arch my back so my chest is thrust further toward him, begging for him to touch them, pull on them, anything. He pinches both my nipples at the same time, and I arch nearly off the table.

"Easy, sweetness." He gentles his touch, bringing me back down from the cliff of desire, and then he pinches them roughly again, revving me back up.

I moan.

"Does it feel good?" he asks in a quiet, low tone.

God, his voice strums something deep inside me. "Mmmm," is all I am able to reply. Every circuit in my brain is overloading.

He teases me some more, grabbing each nipple between his thumb and index finger and rolling them back and forth.

"You like it when I play with your hard nipples, city girl?"

I mutter words, I think. I don't know what words. Just words.

He pinches them harder and pulls, making me cry out in pleasure. "What's that, sweetness?"

"Yes, I love it when you play with my hard nipples. God, it feels so good."

He lets go of them, replacing one hand with his mouth, slurping and sucking my tit while he gropes at the other. Oh my God. My pussy clenches hard like it's directly attached to my chest. His tongue flicks, then he takes my nipple in his mouth and rolls it gently between his teeth.

"Your tits are made for a man to fuck."

I don't even know what that means, so I moan because it sounds fucking hot to me.

Sure, yes, fuck my tits. I bet that's amazing.

Then he's massaging my torso again. Bringing his hands down over my hips, down my legs and back up. I'm so wet I'm leaking onto the towel beneath me. I don't know if I should be embarrassed by that or not. I don't know if nice girls are supposed to get so wet. But I'm not supposed to be a nice girl right now, am I?

Those large hands separate my legs so he can massage the insides of them. But he teases me by avoiding the apex where I'm literally drooling for his attention. A few more minutes and I'm trembling. "Dusty, please."

"Please what?"

"Touch me."

"I am touching you."

"You know what I mean."

"You're the guest. You're going to have to ask for what you want."

Someday, if I'm lucky, I will repay him in kind for this torture. "Cowboy, please touch my pussy."

"Bend your legs," he instructs. I plant my feet flat against the table and bend my legs, spread open for him. Vulnerable in a way I've never known.

"Oh, baby. That's the prettiest pussy I've ever seen."

I blush at the compliment, which is ridiculous.

He dips his fingers through the lips. "So juicy." I squirm when he strokes my clit. "So creamy." He slips a finger inside me. Then two.

"Dusty!" I yell. I'm so thankful we're alone in this house, but I feel like they could probably hear me all the way in Buffalo.

"Yes, baby?"

"Oh, God."

He pumps them inside me, using his thumb to put pressure on my clit. "How about this? Does this feel good?"

The sound that comes out of me is part moan, part prayer.

"I asked you a question. Do you like it when I fuck your tight, wet pussy with my fingers, city girl?"

"Oh, yes," I utter on an exhale. I love it.

"Look at me, Ruby."

I angle my head as he lowers his, forcing me to keep eye contact with him while he puts his mouth on my pussy. It's unbearably intimate. I can't hide behind closed eyes. I can't hide behind the mask of a character I'm pretending to be. It's me. It's him. It's us. Earthy and raw. His tongue is exploring my folds, drinking me.

Oh my God, he's drinking me.

I want to look away when he swirls the pearl of my clit in his mouth. But he holds me captive in his hungry gaze. The connection is too intense. Too much pleasure. Too much sensation.

He moves his fingers just right, hitting the secret spot inside that I've never quite gotten with a toy. I jolt and he pulls his lips off me. "You're so fucking hot, Ruby. I wanted to fuck you as soon as you rounded the corner of that limo."

I squeeze my eyes closed. "I'm going to come!"

"Oh, no, you're not. Not yet." He takes his fingers out of me and rubs my wetness on my breast before he leans down and sucks it into his mouth.

"I think I'm still going to come," I say, the sensation of him tasting my pussy on my tits is so dirty, so nasty, I think it will send me right over.

"I told you not yet. I want you to come when I'm inside you. I want to feel the walls of your pussy clutching around me, milking me as you come all over my dick."

"Then stop talking dirty because you're about to send me over the edge."

He chuckles. "Maybe you need a distraction then." He brings one of my hands to the huge bulge in his pants. God, he's hard as iron in there. I squeeze and his eyes roll back. "Yeah. That's it, sweetness."

That thing is probably going to hurt like hell. I can hardly wait. I want him inside me. I need him inside me. I tug on his waistband, bringing my other hand off the pillow to help. The beast springs free and hits me in the face.

Two hands. I need two hands to hold it. It jumps against my palms, pulsing.

Dusty groans and rips his shirt off his body. His chiseled chest and abs are ridged for my pleasure. The springy hair swirls lightly around his pecs and tapers in a dusting down rock-hard abs until it gets to his perfect cock. The one I'm holding in both hands. Oh my God. I have ideas about what I'm supposed to do with it, but I'm not proficient by any means. I'm going on pure instinct here and hoping I don't screw this up.

I take one hand off so I can see his cock better. It's a perfect shade of pink and so damn thick and long. The bulbous tip is big. Too big. And it's coated in clear precum. My mouth waters. I want that. I want to taste him there. I want to know the texture of him on my tongue, my lips. I've never gone down on anyone before, but I'm hoping enthusiasm will make up for lack of experience because I'm pretty damn excited about getting him in my mouth.

"Like what you see?"

"I think you're perfect."

He leans down, his hand cupping my cheek then delving into my hair. "I can't decide if I want to treat you like glass or fuck you like an animal, sweetness. You revved up a part of me that makes me want to say things to you that a man doesn't say to a lady." He's searching my eyes. What does he see there? "Are you there with me, angel? Do you understand what I'm asking?"

"I don't want you to hold back. Let go with me, Dusty. I don't want to be a lady right now."

"I don't want to offend you or—" He stops talking when I squeeze his dick. "Fair enough. Do you think you can take this big cowboy cock, city girl?"

"I know I can." I hope.

He takes himself in hand and rubs his cock on my lips. "Do you want a taste, darlin'?"

I stick out my tongue and lick the underside of the ridge, letting him coat my lips with the clear fluid. I'm hooked on his taste instantly. He's earthy and clean. It's a weird angle, me laying down and him standing at my head, but I make the most of it and try to get more of him in my mouth.

"God damn. That's good. Oh, baby." He pulls away.

"Hey," I complain.

He pushes his pants all the way off his legs and steps out of them, then he scoops me up off the table, carrying me to that great big bed like I weigh nothing. When I'm in the middle of it, he pins me down, the solid weight of him pushing me into the downy softness below me, the contrast unbearably wonderful.

And then he kisses me.

I can't believe I had his cock in my mouth before he even kissed me, but it doesn't matter much now. His hard cock is digging into my stomach while his tongue tangles with mine. I taste myself on him. I always thought that sounded weird. But it's not. It's hot as fuck.

I've never been kissed so hungrily, so intimately. I pour myself into the kiss, trying to tell him everything I don't have words for. I wrap my legs around his waist, and he moves his hips so his dick slides through my wet heat. We both groan.

"Fuck, you feel so good, darlin'." He moves down, kissing my neck, my tits, my stomach. He rubs his cheek against my mound. "You're so wet for me. I can't wait to feel you tight around my dick."

"How about now?"

"Nah. Busy." He parts my legs and trails his tongue around my inner thighs, always getting closer, but never close enough. When he parts my pussy with his fingers, I brace for more, but he pauses.

"What's wrong?"

"Not a damn thing. I'm just waiting for you to tell me what you want."

Oh. My. God. He's not going to make this easy on me at all, is he?

"Cowboy, I want to ride your tongue."

Dusty

SHE'S THE DEVIL'S DAUGHTER wearing angel white.

I don't know how else to explain the different feelings she's pulling out of me. I want to put her on a pedestal as much as I want to fuck her in the gutter.

I flip us over and roughly bring that sweet pussy to my face. "Then ride me, baby."

I guess she's just as conflicted as I am because the girl who just wanted to ride my tongue is now blushing like a fire engine and frozen in shock.

No matter. I grab two handfuls of that juicy ass and bring her down to my mouth. I love the way she tastes, the slick feel of her on my tongue. I grind her hips until she catches the rhythm and throws back her head.

Her thighs are trembling as I gorge on the feminine feast between her legs. I've always thought I was a good and patient lover. I've enjoyed eating pussy over the years, but it's never been anything like this. Like I can't get enough.

This isn't sex like anything I've ever had.

"Wait. Wait." She's pushing on my chest, putting distance between us. I growl like a damned wolf trying to guard its meal. "You're going to make me come. You said you wanted me to...oh God...You said..."

"Forget what I fucking said. Come on my face, darlin'. You can come on my dick next." This isn't going to be a one and done, that's for damn sure.

Easy, boy. Don't get too caught up.

I squeeze her ass to me again and just gorge on her until she's sobbing my name and goes limp above me. I ain't even sure I'm ready to stop, but she's shivering and shaking, and I need to make sure I didn't just kill the poor girl with pleasure.

She's supple and soft as I roll us to our sides. Her face is slack, her eyelids heavy, and my city girl looks relaxed for the first time since I met her. I did that. I took all her bones and turned them to jelly. Male pride fills me up.

"Am I still alive?" she asks, cracking one eye open.

"I sure as hell hope so. I still have plans for you."

She smiles wryly. "I don't think I can move. I hope you don't need my help."

"You'll move just fine, trust me." The way my girl responds to sex, she'll be up and ready again in a minute or two.

She's not your girl.

I best not get too wrapped up in this. She's leaving in a week.

I lay her flat on her back and nuzzle those pretty tits some more, my dick reminding me that we didn't complete our mission just yet.

I rub my cock against the entrance of her pussy, gathering the juices and teasing us both.

"What do you think, sweetheart? What do want me to do?" I ask coyly, loving the sweet shudder of breath she lets out when I graze her clit.

"What are my choices?"

"One choice really. I'm going to plunge my long, hard cock balls-deep inside your tight wet pussy and fuck you relentlessly until you come all over my dick."

She smiles. "I have condoms in the drawer."

She indicates with her eyes which nightstand, so I reach over and suit up. I want to fuck her raw. I want to fill her with my cum and watch it drip out of her. But that's not how this world works, and I'm fine with latex if it gets me inside the heaven between her legs.

As wet and lax as she is, I don't expect I'll need any more foreplay. But she was tight around my fingers, and I'm hung like a horse. I don't want to hurt the poor girl. I lean down and give her a few more licks, loving the subtle flavors of her.

I pull back. "Do you think you can give me another one, angel?" I have this deep need inside me to see her come again. I suck on that beautiful cunt like a man possessed...again...until she's bucking into my chin and crying out. "God damn, that's a beautiful sight."

I slide back up her body, covering her as she comes down from that high with violent shivers. My cock is probing her pussy, and I can't wait any longer, suddenly thrusting every inch of myself inside her in one go.

I rear back. She's stiff as a board, her eyes wide, and I realize I felt a barrier when I slammed into her.

Fuck. Me.

She's a virgin.

Or she was.

"Ruby? Are you okay?" I hold very still. Damn it, I don't want to break her. She's tight like a vise and every fiber of my being is bursting with pure ecstasy and perfect shame. "Why didn't you tell me?"

She's pursing her lips together so hard they are white. "Are you mad?"

"No!" I yell. Then shake my head and try again. "No," I say, much quieter this time. "I'm just confused. I didn't know. I would have...treated you more carefully."

She whimpers. "You're really fucking big."

Her voice cracks a little on the word big, and I rest my forehead against hers, breathing deep, trying not to fucking move. "Yeah, sweetheart."

I'm a fucking brute is what I am. Practically a giant to her. I grit my teeth against the urge to thrust. Deeper. Harder. That's all I want in this world right now, but I can't. I feel like an ox in a miniature shop. There's too much of me and not enough of her. I can't believe I broke her cherry so roughly. Like a damned clod.

"This is...a little awkward."

"Hey," I catch her eyes with mine. I want to comfort her. I feel like such an asshole. "It's just us. We're as close as two people can be right now. I'm inside you, angel. Nothing that happens in this bed is wrong, okay?"

She nods, but her eyes are shining with unshed tears. "It's starting to hurt less."

"Good. Good." I exhale. "Do you want to stop? I can...pull out." God, please let her say no.

"No. I want to keep going. I wanted it to be you. This is what I want."

"Darlin'." I don't even know how to feel about that. "I could have been gentler. Should have been. I should have made this better for you."

"Well, we're not done, right?"

I bury my nose in her neck, inhaling that sweet, sugary scent of her. I'll never go to the county fair again without thinking of her when I smell the cotton candy. "Nope. We're not done yet."

"So make it good for me now then." She shifts her hips, and I groan.

I'm balls-deep in virgin pussy. She's been saving it for twenty-some years, and it's me she chose to give it to. I've never felt more like a man of worth and more out of my depth at the same time.

I'm not going to rut into her like I want to. I need to give her something sweet to remember. I pull out a little and push back in slowly. Fuck. She feels so amazing. So tight and wet and warm. I wheeze in another few breaths, trying to keep control.

I work in and out of her slowly, letting her feel every single inch of me rubbing against those tight walls inside her body. The tension she's been holding onto from that first, rough thrust starts easing off. She tilts her hips up invitingly. Yeah. That's it.

As I rock into her, building more and more momentum, she starts meeting me thrust for thrust. Her nails dig into my back, spurring me faster, harder. I want to make sure she's into it, not just in pain, so I pull my head back and get a long look into her face.

Her pretty eyes look right into me, and I lose focus for a minute, lost in her. "How you doing, angel?"

She smiles and my heart squeezes in a new, unfamiliar way.

Hell. My fool heart needs to stay in its own lane. I ignore whatever it's trying to tell me and shift the mood back to giving the lady what she came for. "You getting ready to come on my cock? I can hardly wait. You're so fucking tight." I pull out so just the tip is nuzzled between those sweet lips of her cunt before slamming hard back into her.

"Oh, yes," she wails.

"Am I filling you up real good, Ruby? Is this what you wanted? To be stuffed full of me?

"Yes, Dusty. Yes."

God, I'd give anything to rip the fucking rubber off my dick and go at her raw. I want to fill her pussy up with my cum. Paint the damn walls of it white. I want to see myself dripping out of her. I'd love to put a baby in there.

Oh, fuck. That does it. The thought of her walking around the ranch all round with a baby I planted in her jacks me up, and I squeeze her flesh wherever I get a hold of it. I'm growling and snarling now, and her pussy clenches around me like a velvet fist. "That's it. Milk my cock."

"I'm coming. Oh, God." She's so wet now I can feel it trickling down my balls. I don't think I can hold out much longer, but I slow my pace to match the spasms and quivers of her pussy, drawing out her pleasure as long as I can.

When her waves start slowing down, I pick up my pace, grinding into her as the tingle starts in the base of my spine. I get one more flash of fucking a baby into her while I pound inside her as I come right over the edge of bliss.

Chapter Four

Ruby

I roll over, the morning light streaming through the lace curtains. It takes a moment to realize where I am and what I'm doing there. Especially when I move again and muscles I didn't know I had twinge.

Oh, yeah.

I'm not a virgin anymore.

I was well and truly fucked last night.

For the first time in a long time, I accomplished what I set out to do—have a fling that I'll always remember. It would be nice if I'd succeeded at something else, too, but I'll take this for now.

And boy, oh boy, will I always remember having sex with Dusty Cassidy, the hung cowboy.

I wince a little when I move out of bed. Dusty's long gone. I remember him kissing my bare shoulder when he left me before dawn.

I'm not sure what happens next since I'm new at flinging. I'm on board for a week-long tryst if he's up for it. The trick will be not falling for him because everything about him is ovary-exploding. His big, burly body, the way he kisses, his perfect manners, his dedication to his business, the way he looks me right in the eyes and makes me feel special. Seen.

He's totally the kind of guy you bring home to meet the parents, but that will never happen.

But a fling would be awesome.

Charlotte has a big, country breakfast ready for me when I get downstairs.

"What are your plans today, Ruby?" she asks, topping off my coffee.

"I don't know."

"It's perfect weather for horseback riding. You should find Dusty and have him get you set up."

"Oh, I don't know…" …how to ride a horse. "I don't want to bother him. He seems busy."

"It would be good for him to take a break. I'll even pack you a picnic."

Charlotte is not subtle. "What are your plans, Charlotte?"

"In between lunch and supper, I need to try and figure out the new reservation software. I just want to use a notebook, but Dusty insists we need a fancy computer setup."

"It will make things easier in the long run."

"If I can ever figure it out."

"Can I see it after breakfast?"

"You're on vacation."

I keep at her until she agrees and after we clear the table, I get behind the front desk and check out their system. "Oh, Charlotte, you can figure this one out for sure." It's a very streamlined version of what I use at work. "Here, let me show you."

I spend half an hour with her until she shoos me out the door, thanking me over and over. It wasn't a bad way to spend a morning. I liked feeling useful.

I find Dusty out behind the barn sawing wood on a sawhorse. I'm suddenly awkward and shy, remembering how it felt last night to be naked with him. To be pinned by all that hot, hard weight.

"Good morning, angel. You sleep well?"

My God, he's beautiful. He's shirtless and sweaty and I'm jealous of the damned sweat clinging to his skin. His massive tree trunk arms cross over his chest, and he grins at me like he knows exactly what I'm thinking about. Like there's a cartoon bubble above my head showing me fantasizing about tracing the deep trenches of his abs with my tongue. That his tight cowboy jeans don't hide the bulge I know is there. I blink back my thoughts. "I slept like a baby."

"You, ah...feeling okay?"

What he doesn't say, I can read clearly in the cartoon bubbles above his head. *Are you sore? Are you emotionally okay? Did I make your first time memorable?* Seriously, the guy is super sweet for someone who says the things he does in bed.

I can feel my blush climbing my cheeks. "Yeah. Last night was wonderful."

Dusty has a delectable dimple that pops out and makes me swoony. We're in this weird, awkward stage. He bends over to grab his water bottle, and when he takes a big drink, the sight of his throat working is somehow sexy too.

"Do you think you'll have time to take me riding later?"

He spit-takes his water, and I curse my stupid, big mouth.

"Horses! I meant horseback riding. Charlotte suggested it. She's making a basket. A picnic in it." I stop talking and count to three, hoping to make more sense this time. "She's making us a picnic basket."

"Sure, city girl. We can go riding. You must not get many chances in Los Angeles."

No, not many.

But how hard can it be? You see kids doing it all the time. You just have to sit on it and hold on, right? I know how to sit.

Fifteen minutes later, I'm staring at a huge animal in front of me. Oh my God. I had no idea horses were so big. I mean, I've seen them from afar or on a screen. But this close. Holy moly.

"This here is Gemini. Sweet girl. She'll take good care of you." He's cinching things and Gemini is clearly in love with him.

But she's giving me the stink-eye.

"I figure we'll ride down to the river. Not too far today. You...ah...might be a bit sore."

Oh my God. I'm blushing again. *Act like you're fine.* "Sounds great."

"You sure you want to do this? You look a little nervous."

Act like you are fine. "It's just been awhile. I'm fine."

I build a character in my head. One who was practically born on a horse. She knows exactly what she's doing and is fearless around the big beasts. Only as soon as I try to get on, Gemini bolts forward, and I miss the saddle, falling back into Dusty's arms.

Luckily, he's perfect at everything, including rescuing dumb city girls. He grins and kisses me square on the mouth. "Awhile, huh? How long exactly?"

I shrug. "A few years...since I've been on a carousel." I bury my face in his neck as he whoops out a great big laugh. "I'm such a moron. I was trying to impress you, I guess."

"Darlin', I thought I showed you last night how impressed I am with you. But if we need to do a replay, I'm happy to oblige."

"You can put me down."

"Now that'd be a damn shame. I like holding you."

"You don't think I'm an idiot?"

"Not everyone was born on a ranch, sweetness. I've been around horses my whole life, so I know my way around them. But there's no shame in not knowing something you've never tried."

"Thank you, for not making me feel worse than I already do. The only animals I've been around are predatory casting directors."

He frowns at that, but quickly changes back to the Dusty I know. "Let's get you set up. This time, I'll help you. Seems like I get to be part of one more of your firsts."

Dusty

"THAT ONE IS AN ELEPHANT."

I close one eye, but still don't see it. "Which one?"

Ruby points to the cloud to the left of the one we just decided was a cupcake. Well, I decided it was a cupcake, she decided it was a red velvet cupcake with brandied frosting on top.

"I still don't see it." I roll to my side and prop my head on my elbow. I'd rather look at her anyway. We've been watching clouds since we finished our fried chicken and potato salad picnic. I don't normally take the whole afternoon for lunch, but we finished a lot of wine too. It's probably been too long since I gazed at the sky. I've been so caught up in building my business, I forgot to remember why I want the dream so bad.

Ruby's not used to slowing down either. But she's looking real pretty on this blanket, the sun catching glints in her brown hair making it look red. I want to ask her what she meant earlier, about the casting directors, but I'm not sure that's wise. It might have been just a little joke, but I have a feeling it's more involved than that. And I don't want to bring up bad memories for her.

It's been in the news so much lately, the rotten things happening to women in Hollywood. Well, everywhere really. When I think of someone taking advantage of her, it feels like someone is squeezing my heart in a fist. Of any woman. But especially her.

But who am I to delve into her past? I'm just her summer cowboy. Last night was amazing, and this day is looking like it might turn into another amazing night. But we're so different. And I don't have time for a relationship and she doesn't have time for a small-time resort owner. She's in Los Angeles for a reason. Big dreams. There's nothing like that for her here, that's for sure.

And I've been down that road before. Saw everything I needed to see on it.

But my gut won't rest until I know. She can always tell me to mind my own business. "What did you mean earlier? About the casting directors?"

"Oh, you don't want to hear my sob story."

I reach for her hand. "You don't need to tell me if you don't want to. I don't want to pry. But I am interested."

She bites her lip. "I was up for a movie role a couple of years ago. It wasn't the lead or anything, but it was a bigger supporting role than anything I'd been able to get close to. Anyway, I was running my lines in the casting director's office when he kissed me." Her forehead crinkles, and her eyes concentrate on something in the distance. "The scene didn't have a kiss in it. He just grabbed me and started kissing me. I tried to push him off me, but it took a few minutes. He told me...he told me that prettier girls were up for the role, but if I gave him a blow job, it was mine. That I should be lucky he liked chubby girls—that a girl my size didn't have too many options and I should really think about it before I said no."

If she tells me his name, I will find him and kill him. I don't even know where to start responding. Should I tell her that she's not chubby? Hell, I don't know. Whatever she is, though, is perfect. But maybe that's the wrong thing to say. Maybe it's not about her looks at all. Maybe it's just the idea that a man who had power over her was using it to crush her self-esteem.

"Anyway," she starts again as if we were talking about the weather, "he stood between me and the door. Told me he could destroy my career. That I wouldn't be able to sell gyno cream much less act in a movie unless I got on my knees."

"Did you?" I ask and immediately regret it. It's not my business if she did. It doesn't change how much I like her or anything. If she did it, she felt she had to. And that's just heartbreaking, really.

"No, I was able to escape. But I haven't gotten many callbacks since. It might just be that I'm not really that good, you know? But," she shrugs, "he might have followed through. It doesn't matter."

"What do you mean it doesn't matter? Ruby, no man has the right to threaten a woman or ask for sexual favors in exchange for a job. That piece of shit shouldn't have done that to you."

She throws her arm over her eyes. I don't know if it's because of the sun or if she's hiding tears. "It happens a lot. It's sort of the price you pay, I guess."

"It ain't right, what he did. Promise me something."

"What?"

"Promise me you won't ever water yourself down just because someone can't handle you at 100 proof."

She sits up on her elbows. "Maybe sometimes dreams come and go. Or they change."

"Yeah, well, right now my dream is to find that snake and remove his rattler."

Chapter Five

Ruby

Dusty hasn't spoken for a few minutes and I think I ruined everything.

I'm so stupid. Who talks about sexual assault on a sexy date?

Everything was perfect before that. The horses are tied to a tree, shaded and happy. The river gurgles over rocks gently. It's warm but not oppressive, the breeze keeping us cool. There are birds and wildflowers everywhere the eye can see. What would it be like to live in a place where everything is so wild and free?

I'm desperate to change the subject. I point to the sky again. "Do you see the elephant yet?"

"Nope."

It actually doesn't look like an elephant anymore anyway.

He sits up. All his muscles are rigid and tight. He's lost that laid-back and flirty feeling.

I have cockblocked myself. Because of course I have. When do I do anything right?

Sometimes, I think I should have just blown that creep on his casting couch. I didn't want my first time with a man to be like that, but maybe I'm too straight-laced. It's just sex, right? I could have forwarded my career instead of killing it. For what, ten minutes? I'm supposed to be an actress. I could have pretended to like it, couldn't I?

But no. My principles wouldn't allow me to, and my principles suck at paying the bills.

There probably was no right choice to make because it was an impossible situation. But I'm tired of always being empty-handed. It isn't working for me in Hollywood, and it sure as heck isn't going to work for me in Pair-a-Dice.

What am I even doing here? I should just tell Dusty let's call it a day and head back to the ranch. I'll read in my room and ask for a tray to be brought up for supper. And then tomorrow, head back home.

But...that's not what I want. I want to have this week. This one measly week. I may never have sex again if my history of bad dates continues. This might be my best and only chance at an affair. I have no competition for Dusty right now—I'm the only woman under fifty on this ranch. He likes me. I like him. And while I don't have anything to judge it against, I'm pretty sure last night was as amazing as it gets. He certainly didn't complain.

Can I salvage this day?

Get into character, girl.

What would a sexually confident woman do? I give an exaggerated sigh and strike a pose that arches my back enticingly. At least, I hope enticingly. I imagine the silhouette of a woman on the mud flaps of a big rig. That's sexy right?

I might be hopeless.

Say something.

"I haven't been swimming in a river since I was a kid." I sigh again. "Too bad I didn't bring a suit."

One thing I appreciate about acting is not having to write my own lines. I'm obviously not good at writing convincing dialogue.

He turns his head toward me, taking in my pose, I think. At least focusing on my breasts. I can see the wheels turning in his head. "It's a pretty nice swimming hole too. I didn't bring a suit either." He inclines his head like, "Isn't that just too bad?"

"Whatever should we do?" I ask on an exaggerated question. "We both want to go swimming. We're all alone here. But we don't have suits to change into."

Dusty looks at me for a long time. Maybe too long? His jaw relaxes. "Well, we could always swim in the suits God gave us."

I blink, pretending I'm surprised. "I don't know...I suppose we've already seen each other naked. So..."

He smiles and my heart trips all over itself. Cowboy smiles are a thing of beauty.

I'm so glad he was my first. I'm glad I ran out of that director's office. I'm glad my dates never made it to my bedroom. Dusty is the perfect memory. I'll treasure last night for the rest of my days.

Dusty stands and pulls me up. Then we stare at each other. Like...what now? I was good at talking the talk, but can I...dare I? Dusty grabs the bottom of his shirt and pulls it off, the fabric rolling up over his muscled torso. He wads it casually in his hands, then tosses it to the picnic blanket.

Wow. He's just...wow.

His skin is drum-tight over row after row of perfectly sculpted abs. Thick arms bulge with meaty, rounded muscles. His wide shoulders could move a house, but it's his torso that I'm strangely attracted to. The way his wide lateral muscles taper down a trim waist into the waistband of his jeans. He quirks his eyebrows at me, teasing out a smile. And then his hand slides to his buckle.

I swallow hard, my attention raptly focused on that hand.

"You okay, Ruby?"

I nod. Sure, I'm okay. How could I not be okay? The hottest man I've ever seen is undoing his belt buckle. Slowly. Then he unbuttons his fly—his thick, rock-hard cock swelling up the front of his blue boxer briefs. He pulls his pants down, somehow stepping out of his boots without the falling down mess that I would be if I tried that maneuver.

He's huge. Everywhere, but I'm not looking at anything else but the bulge. Then he steps out of his underwear. I can't breathe. He wraps one fist around the hardy base of his cock, squeezes it and slides down. I'm on fire watching him handle himself.

"You gonna strip?"

Now I'm self-conscious. But his hard-on is for me, so he must want to see me naked as much as I want to see him. I slide my shirt up and over my head before unhooking my bra and letting it fall.

He whistles. "Holy shit. Your tits are amazing. Fucking amazing."

Well, that gives me a little more confidence. I bring my shorts and panties down together, toeing off my shoes before I try to get them all the way off. Now we're both naked, standing outdoors and in the sunlight.

"Do that again," I boldly say. "With your hand."

"This, darlin'?" He grabs himself again. Then he strokes himself lazily.

"Yes, that. I like it."

His wry grin doesn't even faze me. "You like watching me touch myself? You want me to keep doing it?"

I nod. "Does that make me perverted?" The sun catches the glint of precum on the tip of his cock and my mouth waters.

"If it does, you're in good company." He glides up and down again. "You keep looking at me like that and we're not going swimming."

I make like I'm going to run. "Last one there is a rotten egg!"

I don't make it two steps before Dusty catches me around my middle and throws me over his shoulder like I weigh twenty pounds instead of...more. He smacks my ass a few times when I protest, so I smack his round, firm ass right back. We make it to the river pretty fast.

Wait.

"Dusty, don't you dare!"

He wades right in and takes us down into the chilly water. I come up sputtering.

"I don't dare what, city girl?"

He's laughing at my outrage, so I barrel into him and dunk him this time. The water is freezing, but Dusty's slick skin is still warm, so I drape myself over him as he wades us further into the swimming hole.

I love touching him, so I indulge myself, running my hands all over the hard planes of his body.

He wraps my legs around his waist, smooshing my tits against his steel torso. "Your nips could cut glass. You cold or turned on?"

I rub my chest against him. "Both."

Dusty cups one of my breasts, my flesh overflowing his hand. When he brings his mouth down to it, I can't help but gasp and arch my back. "I love how sensitive your tits are." He sucks as much of me into his mouth as he can and moans around me, kneading my ass.

His hand slides into the crevice and he starts to use his fingers to explore my pussy, starting just above my opening and stopping just short of my clit. I gasp, gulping air like a guppy out of water.

"Easy, angel." He pushes two fingers into my pussy and begins to slowly fuck me with them, twisting and pressing against my G-spot, and then pulling them in and out. Over and over, all the while watching my face. "Oh, baby. You're so close, aren't you?"

I can only whimper my response. All my world has become the tight space around his fingers.

"You're so hot and wet. You might have been a virgin just yesterday, but you're a woman now, aren't you? Say it. Tell me you want me to make you come."

The spinning in my head increases. My back arches and pussy clenches around his beefy fingers. I can't concentrate on anything but the delicious waves of pleasure between my legs. I'm grinding up to get more of his fingers inside me. My nerves are red hot, screaming for release. "Make me come, Dusty. God, please."

I cry out, grinding against his hand. I ride it hard, desperate for the violent orgasm I know is coming.

"My naughty city girl," he whispers. "Such a bad girl, letting her cowboy fingerfuck her outside where anyone could see. Bad, bad girl."

"Oh, God," I plead.

The fiery pressure builds and builds until white hot ecstasy jolts from my pussy through every other part of my body. Maybe even my soul. My hips start to buck violently.

"That's it, my dirty angel. Come all over my hand."

I sob as the fierce release wracks my body until I'm worn out and trembling. I bury myself in his neck. clutching his biceps, holding on for dear life as the orgasm winds down.

Slowly, I become aware of the cold water, the hot sun overhead, the sounds of the winds rustling the wild grasses. The thumping in my head slows and I shiver. "God, I need a nap."

He chuckles, the rumble low in his throat. "I don't think so."

I pull back and look up at him. His face is tense, stern. But his eyes are anything but cold. No, they burn warm like the sun. "Dusty?"

"You're not sleeping yet. Not until I've fucked the angel sweetness right out of you."

Dusty

MY VISION IS CLOUDED in a red haze. I reluctantly pull my fingers out of that sweet pussy and use both hands to hold her ass as I walk us out of the river back to the blanket.

I'm on fire for her. I want to be inside her more than I've ever wanted any damn thing in my life. I can't think. I don't care if I'm stepping on jagged rocks or sharp grass.

I don't even know what I'm saying. Fuck the angel sweetness out of her? What does that even mean? But I want the fiery devil girl inside to come and play. I want her raw and primitive and worshiping my cock.

I lay her down and spread her legs. She's staring at me like she doesn't know me, and hell if I even recognize myself right now. I get on my knees and spread her legs wide, staring at that sweet pussy that just spasmed around my fingers so hard.

"Mine," I growl and lean down, pressing my lips against her soaked center, breathing her in heavily. A slow spasm of pleasure rolls through my body at her scent. *Mine.*

"You're a filthy girl, Ruby," I murmur against her soaking wet flesh.

She opens her mouth, maybe to protest, but nothing comes out except a squeak as I start fucking her with my tongue. Her flavors are so rich, intoxicating. I plunge fast and deep into her wetness. Her shaking fingers slip through my hair, pulling me harder against her as I make her my meal.

Sloppy. Wet. Tangy. Sweet. I want to drown in her juices.

"I'm gonna fuck you," I say into her muff. "Gonna stuff you full with my thick cock."

She grasps my hair hard. "Yes!"

"You're gonna worship my cock. It's gonna make you feel every inch of it in ways you never dreamed of. It's going to fucking own you." I go back down and she grinds against my face. I'm covered in her, and I still want more. "I'm going to fuck you so hard and so good that you're never going to be able to come without thinking about me."

Mine.

This is going to be good. Unlike anything I've ever felt before. Something about the two of us is just explosive.

She starts chanting my name, and her whole body tenses. I get another rush of her girl-cum as she orgasms hard against my face.

I can't wait anymore. I move up and cover her body with mine, shoving my dick inside her with one long, slow glide. Her eyes widen with every inch I forcefully push. I'm panting hard when I bottom out, and I rest my forehead against hers and let the rush overtake me.

I'm still horny as fuck, but the second I slid home, something changed. She's tight, slick, and warm. I want to stay here forever.

I thrust inside her in slow, constant, and thorough strokes.

I clutch her ass, pushing against her stomach, trying to get as deep as I can. Her legs wrap around my waist, pulling me in tighter, her feet digging into my ass. I clutch at her tit and proceed to pound her even harder.

She tries to shut her eyes, but I grab her hair, pulling it lightly so she'll keep her eyes on me. "Don't fucking shut me out now. You look at me while you come. It's me that's taking you there." I feel barbaric and I don't care. There is nothing civilized about the way we fuck. Her face tightens as I watch her come again, her eyes on me. It's not a violent orgasm like before. It's a long, slow pulse. I groan when her pussy squeezes my dick, pulling me in deeper. Her drenched pussy gives me another shock of pleasure

A growl builds up from my chest and into my throat. My thrusting grows frantic and my grunts desperate. My lips sear her with a scorching kiss. My heavy cock lets go, pushing bursts of cum inside her with every jump. I pour myself into her, demanding that she take it all. Take all of me.

"I'm filling you up, angel. Filling you so full of my cum."

She sobs as another orgasm rocks her body, pulling even more out of me.

That's when I realize we didn't use any birth control.

Chapter Six

Ruby

I'm feeling pretty fucking good right now.

I'm not sure how many orgasms I've had at Pair-a-Dice Ranch, but it's been a pretty good run. I love the weight of the cowboy on top of me. He's solid and real, a little slick with sweat. Why do I never meet men like Dusty in Los Angeles? There are more men there, you'd think my chances would be better.

I can't believe, just yesterday, my hottest fantasy was a pretentious businessman in a suit gently removing my virginity after a four-course meal and cocktails. This is so much better. Getting fucked outside, in the sun, in the water. Having a man completely lose his mind because he's so in lust with you.

And when we're not having sex? He's courteous and interested. He knows how to build things with his hands. Can tame huge horses with the tone of his voice. He's just...made of substance.

"Are you okay? I was a little rough."

I lick his shoulder because I can. "Why can't I have met you in Los Angeles, cowboy? I'm only going to be here for a few days, and I'm already going to miss you."

Oh God. Do I sound needy? Like I'm reading too much into this fling? I should have kept my mouth shut.

He freezes, his whole body going rigid. He rolls over and off me quickly. "Shit. Tell me you're on the pill, darlin'. I just rode you bareback."

Oh no. The blood drains from my face, and if I weren't lying down, my knees would have given out. "I'm sorry," I stammer. "No. I should have..."

"It's not your fault." But he looks mad. Tense. A quick and unwelcome change from the savage man who'd just plundered me. "I'm going to go rinse off. We should head back."

He's gone before I can even respond. I feel dirty somehow. And stupid. What was I thinking? Why wasn't I thinking? He doesn't seem like the type to sleep with a million women, but I hardly know him. I didn't protect myself. I know better than that.

Not to mention the risk I just took with pregnancy.

My hand immediately covers my stomach. That's exactly what I need. A baby, right? I can barely take care of myself in the city, much less a child.

What seemed so fun and freeing a few minutes ago now feels sordid and irresponsible. I'm suddenly very aware of my nakedness in a way I wasn't while a man was inside me. In a way that makes me feel shameful. Is that why he bolted so fast to the river? Because I'm something he wants to wash off? A mistake he needs to hide the evidence of?

I don't love this feeling as I yank my T-shirt back on. It's starting to occur to me that I'm not the only one to blame here. I didn't cart myself out of the river and on to this blanket. I didn't tell him I was going to fuck him until he couldn't get turned on again without thinking of me. I didn't come inside him and then ask him if he'd remembered to make sure he wouldn't get pregnant. He has more experience at these things than I do, and he knows it. We're in this mess together.

But that's not how life works. If there's a mess, it will be up to me to take care of it. It will be me taking care of it for eighteen years while Dusty goes on seducing women in rivers and impregnating them at will.

Damn it. I stuff my legs into my shorts. I really want to clean up in the river, too, but I'll be damned if I go down there now. Not while he's washing the scent of me off his body and blaming me for being stupid enough to get seduced by a big, dumb cowboy. If he thinks—

"I'm sorry, Ruby. I shouldn't have stormed off like that."

I nearly jump out of my skin. "Dusty, I...I didn't hear you come back."

"Well, then I'm sorry for startling you too."

I look away while he gets dressed.

An angry ball of tears is working its way up my throat, and I do my best to swallow it back down.

"Look, I'm sorry that I didn't protect you," he says. "I let my passion control me instead of my head, and I put us in a precarious situation."

Air shudders through my lungs, and my lip trembles. Damn it. I do not want to cry.

"I won't make that mistake again, okay. Please don't be upset with me."

Mistake. That's what this is. Was. I have a feeling there isn't an "is" anymore.

"I'd like to head back to the ranch. I need a shower before dinner."

And it be will a cold day in hell before I let him see me cry.

Dusty

THE RIDE BACK TO THE ranch was awful quiet. She was probably kicking herself for getting involved with a big, dumb ox. I know I hurt her feelings. I know I'd like to make it up to her, but it's probably best that we just let it lie now. When I'm thinking clearly, I'll approach her about the possible pregnancy. Until then, I need to stay far, far away from the enticing Ms. Ruby Grant.

We don't belong together. She's a city girl and I'm a cowboy. We're nothing alike, and pretending we belong together is a huge mistake, no matter how good the sex is. And damn, is it good.

At supper, she joins us at the table fresh as a daisy in a pretty summer dress. I allow myself one good look before I try to keep my eyes on my plate. She's so pretty it makes my heart ache.

The sound of eating and conversation around me stops, and I panic that maybe I said that out loud. Everyone is staring at me. "What?" I ask around a forkful of potatoes.

Aunt Charlotte bats my arm. "Don't talk with your mouth full. I raised you better than that."

I swallow. "Why is everyone looking at me?"

My ranch hand and good friend Carter shakes his head the same as he did when were kids and I made a fool of myself for Lisa Langston at the eighth-grade dance. "The lady asked you a question." He tilts his head toward the only lady at our table I'm not related to.

"I'm sorry, Ruby. I didn't hear you."

She blinks at me a few times. "I asked what you majored in at college."

"Business."

The crew looks around awkwardly as she asks me a few more small talk questions, and I answer with one-word answers and desperately try to avoid her gaze. I'm polite but not overly friendly, and it hasn't escaped anyone's notice that something is not quite right.

"Did you two enjoy your ride today?" my aunt asks.

I choke on my water and Carter pounds on my back. Hard. Harder than necessary, I reckon. He's no dummy. He knows something is up, and he's gonna give me hell about it later.

"It was my first time, but I think I got the hang of it," Ruby answers.

I dare a glance at her and find that her expression isn't angry. She meant that as a private joke between us. Now would be my chance to flirt back harmlessly. But there is nothing harmless about flirting with

Ruby. Not anymore. So I look back at my plate and eat my dinner like it's my second job.

"I'd like to go over some plans with you after supper, Dusty," Carter says in a tone that means he's probably also going to kick my ass. And don't I just deserve that?

"Sure thing, Hoss."

We help clear the table and clean the kitchen and then Carter and I head out to the barn.

"What's going on with you and Ruby, asshole?"

Should I tell him the truth? Do I know the truth?

"Nothing. She's a guest."

"Bullshit."

"You kiss your mother with that mouth?"

"I do. And I'm gonna kick your ass with this foot. What the hell, man? You're building your empire here. You don't have time to chase pussy and you sure as hell don't have time to ruin your reputation by fucking your customers."

I clench my fist, but don't hit him. I know when I'm being baited. I don't need to defend Ruby's honor because he only said it to make me defend her honor.

"It was just a one-time thing. It's over now."

Carter pulls out a few sugar cubes he'd pilfered from the kitchen for Gemini. "Did you bother telling that to Ruby?"

"Ruby is a big girl and she knows what is and what isn't."

"Asshole, you best just talk to me before we start sounding like a couple of chicks with me begging you to share your feelings. Just spill."

I lean against a post and thunk my head against it. "I like her. A lot." The jerk doesn't say anything, so I have to keep talking. "She's funny and smart and beautiful. Sexy as fuck."

"So what is the problem?"

"She lives in Los Angeles and I live here. She doesn't know anything about ranch life and I sure as hell ain't moving to a big city. She wants to be an actress. There's not a big call for them out here. It's like Farrah all over again."

And there it is. The thing I've been avoiding thinking about. It's out there now.

"Ruby is nothing like Farrah."

Farrah and Carter never got along. None of my friends or family liked her, for that matter. "This isn't the time to discuss it."

"You know what? Maybe it is. Farrah was a manipulator and user. She didn't love anyone but herself and she almost ruined you."

I blow out a long breath. "She just wanted different things."

"Yeah. Like coke and diamonds and parties. Is Ruby into any of those things?"

No. "How do I know? We only just met."

"Fine. If you don't want her, I'd like to ask her out."

My blood pressure rises, but I keep my cool. He's still baiting me. He's been dating Marissa from the pub for months now. "Suit yourself."

"Really. Who knows? Maybe she doesn't even like her city life. Maybe she'd love a chance to settle down here and raise a little family with me. Or one of the other guys. And if not, hopefully I can get a fuck out of it before she goes, right?"

I've got him across the barn against a wall with my arm pressing against his throat before I know what I'm doing. "Shut up, Carter." I let up on his throat. "Don't push me about this."

"How do you know she doesn't belong here if you don't ask?

"Farrah hated—"

"She's not like Farrah. Even I know that, and I've talked to her just a couple times. Farrah never wanted to settle down in Wyoming. She was never satisfied. Even when she got out, she wasn't satisfied. She killed herself with those drugs because she couldn't outrun herself no matter where she went. And she tried to take you down with her."

I let go of Carter and stroll over to Gemini. "I was careless today. Forgot protection."

"Jesus Christ, you really are a dumb fuck, ain't ya?" But he doesn't push it. Nobody talks much about the fact that Farrah was pregnant with my baby when she died from a heroin overdose. She'd called me that morning. Told me she was pregnant and scared, and I drove to the city to rescue her. Bring her back. Only she was dead when I got there.

"Ruby's not Farrah."

"I don't want to hurt her by pretending we could have a future together."

She wanted a fling. I gave her one. But that's all of myself that I have to give.

Chapter Seven

Ruby

Waking up this morning was so different from yesterday morning. I'm still sore, but it doesn't feel delicious.

I'd hoped he would come to my room last night, after all was said and done. And maybe we could talk. Or maybe even more. But at least we could salvage something. But I've spent the morning trying to track him down and he clearly doesn't want to be found. It seems I'm always a step behind.

I know lots of men ghost on women, but I didn't think he was the type. And it's his ranch. His house. Is he really planning on just avoiding me until I leave?

Part of me wants to talk to him now and give him a piece of my mind for being so immature. Surely, the big tough cowboy can't be afraid of a little girl, can he? The big lug.

But I don't want to be too desperate.

I don't know what to do, so I find myself dialing my roommate Katie. She's got a lot of experience with men. Wait. That sounds bad. She has more experience than I do with men.

Oh, who am I kidding?

She burns through men like a California wildfire in August.

Miracle of miracles, I get a signal.

"I've been trying to call you," she says.

"Reception is spotty here. Let me tell you a little story..." I fill her in, with broad strokes. I'm not comfortable sharing anything too intimate with her. Maybe someday, when it's not so fresh and raw.

I definitely don't tell her about the sex with no condom.

"I really like him, Katie. I thought we could be friends. You know. With benefits. He's so nice and you can tell a lot about a guy by the way he treats animals. He's just got this gentle, yet totally alpha, energy going on. Like you know he's the safest person to be near in an emergency."

"But how does he fuck?"

Like a god. "I have no complaints."

"Well, if he's as good looking as you say he is…"

"He totally is. I'd take him over Model Mark in 2A any day." I've had a small crush on Model Mark for almost a year. The only thing he's ever said to me was, "You dropped your light bill," at the mailbox, but I lived on that for a week or two.

"Then he just wanted to get his dick wet, Ruby. You said yourself you're the only woman under fifty and unrelated to him for miles around."

"I'm fine with a fling. Really. But the way he was yesterday, I guess I just thought we were more like…a vacation fling than a one-night stand kind of fling."

"Look, you know I like you a lot. But guys are different. They don't care about your good personality. They want hot chicks. And if none are available, they make do."

Make do.

Ouch.

That doesn't really feel like Dusty, but then neither did his disappearing act. I guess I don't know him well enough to judge.

"What are you even doing there, Ruby? You should have come home and gone back to work instead of running around having sex with hot cowboys."

I lean back on the tower of pillows. I will so miss this bed when I get home. My futon is crappy. Well, Katie's futon. I swapped beds with her because she was having back problems last year. I thought it was just temporary until her back healed, but I haven't asked to trade back and she hasn't offered.

"I needed a break."

"Well, we need to pay the rent."

I sit up. "The rent?"

"Landlord says he'll evict us in three days if we don't catch up."

"I left my half on the counter before I left. Why didn't it get paid?"

"I'm short this month."

Every month. "Can you borrow some?"

"You know I can't. I tried to pick up more hours, but they just weren't available."

Sure, she did. Katie probably didn't even work all the shifts she was scheduled for. "What do you want me to do? I'm in Wyoming. I paid my share."

"God, you're so selfish. Just enjoy your little vacation and don't worry about getting evicted. Just leave me here to deal with it."

I bite back my ingrained response to apologize. This isn't my problem. I paid my share. I usually pay more than my share, and she always makes me feel like I'm not. It's always like this.

"Yeah, I guess I will. It's time for my mani-pedi and facial. Ta-ta." I hang up and throw myself back onto the pillows. No. If I stay here, I'll start crying or worse, I'll call her back and apologize and figure out how to wire money to her. I slip on my tennis shoes and leave my phone behind.

Dusty

FOR THE FIRST TIME since I bought the ranch at auction, I'm not excited about my chores. Usually, I get a sense of pride, and I enjoy working with the animals, breaking a sweat, and knowing I'm doing the work that I'm meant to do. But today, everything is a drudge.

Pretty much everyone with half a brain has turned the other way when they see me coming. That's new too. My crew and I are more like family than boss and employees, but I guess I look like the devil and I feel like him too.

I round the corner of an outbuilding and almost turn the other way. Maybe she didn't see me. I don't think she does, she hasn't lifted her head. She's sitting on the ground, her knees up to her chest.

Shit. She's crying. Her tears gut me. I can't stand it. I'd do anything to make sure she never cries again.

"Ruby?"

She looks up and her eyes are rimmed in red. When the recognition that it's me passes over her features, her eyes go dark. "Go away. Please go away."

"Ruby, angel. What's wrong? Are you hurt?"

She scrambles up, brushing twigs and dirt off herself. "I really can't do this right now. Please, if you have a shred of decency you'll just turn around and let me retreat in peace. I'll go up to my room. You won't even have to see me. You don't have to skulk around your property trying to avoid me."

"Ruby..." I don't know what to say. What to do. She asked me to leave, but is that what she wants? I don't want to leave her alone, but I'm probably not the best one to offer her comfort. Then it hits me that maybe I'm the reason for her tears.

Fuck. Me.

I stand there too long, not saying anything. Not taking any action. Just feeling my heart crack into a million pieces at the thought that I could hurt her when all I want to do is protect her. But I guess I stand there too long.

She turns and walks the other way.

"Ruby, please. Wait." I catch up to her. "Please tell me what is wrong."

"Why do you even care?"

"You think I don't care?"

"I think you've been running scared from me since you realized that there might be consequences to being my first lover. But don't worry about it. I'll handle whatever comes my way without you."

"Ruby."

"I get it, okay? You think I'm clingy or whatever because it was my first time. That if you're too nice to me, I might have expectations. That if I get pregnant, I'll try to trap you or whatever. But I was prepared to have an affair. I might have wanted your companionship, sure. But I'm not angling for a relationship. And I certainly don't want to be pregnant, much less force you into anything."

"Then why are you crying?"

She narrows her eyes even as she wipes the tears from them. "You think these tears are for you? Trust me, I don't want to have anything more to do with you than you want from me. I'm not wailing with sadness over losing what I never even had." She's vibrating with anger. "Deep down, I think you're probably a nice guy. Or you want to be. But you're not interested in anything more than any other man I've met since I left home. Which is a shame because I think we could have been friends."

I feel about two inches tall. "I do want to be friends."

I want more than that. I want to be her goddamn hero. The guy she turns to, to slay whatever dragons are making her cry. I want to be the one she seeks out when she's happy and when she's sad. I want...just more. But I was too scared of my own feelings to realize it and now that I see it, it's too late. I'm more of a zero than hero. I disappointed her, and I'll have to live with that every day.

"Look, Dusty, if you're just feeling sorry for me, then save it, okay? I don't need it. It's okay that you don't care. I'm just a random lay that overstayed her welcome."

"You're a guest in my home. You didn't overstay."

She shrugs and it's such a lonely action. I can see it. She's given up on just about everyone. "I'll let you know what happens with...well...if I get pregnant. But I don't expect anything from you."

The idea that she might at this very minute be carrying my child gives me a hard-on. An unwelcome one. I really am a shitty person.

"You're more than a random lay. You know that."

She raises her brow. "Seriously? You don't have to make me feel good about myself. I wanted to have sex with you and I did. I don't care if I was a random lay or not."

"I care." I palm her shoulders. "I care about you too much."

"*You* are too much. I'm going back to the house now."

"Do you think that it hasn't been killing me to stay away from you? That I'm not already addicted to the way you taste and the sound of your laugh or the way you moan when I'm inside you?"

She pulls back like I slapped her.

Man up, cowboy.

"You're right. I did run. It wasn't because I don't care. It's because I care too much. I know I don't have a future with you. I can't give you what you need here."

"What do you know about what I need?"

"You want to be an actress. You live in Hollywood. You probably like fancy cars and fashion and parties and I've got nothing to offer you."

She huffs out a rueful laugh. "You think I'm a party girl?" She plops down on the grass, so I join her. "I got in a fight with my roommate. I'm pretty sure we're being evicted because I wasn't there to pay more than my share of the rent on our crappy little apartment."

"Why do you have to pay more than your half?"

She sighs. "At first, I thought I was helping a friend, but Katie's been leeching off me for a long time. She's just using me." She picks random blades of grass. "Sometimes I feel like everyone in LA only wants to use me up and throw me away."

And she thought I was one of them. Because of the way I acted. "I know how you feel. It's hard to find good people these days. That's why I work so hard to make this place work. For my friends, my family. Sometimes everyone else seems out for themselves."

"I think you care. About people."

"I think you do too. Maybe too much, sounds like."

"Maybe too much."

We're quiet for a few minutes, just listening to the breeze whistle through the windbreak and a cow lowing in the pasture. "Do you think you'd give me a second chance? To be a better friend to you than I was."

She gazes into my eyes like she's trying to read me. "If you tell me why you ran so fast."

I pull my hat off my head. "You don't ask for much, do you? Just filet myself open for you?"

"If you don't want to tell—"

"I thought I was in love once."

That shuts her up.

"Her name was Farrah. She went to high school with Carter and me. She was a troubled girl, always. And so damned restless. Wanted to be a model. Wanted the good life, she always said. She kept moving away to the city and coming back, each time a little skinnier, as little more rough around her edges. I tried to give her a good home base. Not pen her in. That was before I bought this place. I had a small house in Buffalo." Ruby covers my big paw with her dainty hand. Support. Reassurance. It sure feels nice. "The last time she left, she was gone a month when she called me one day out of the blue crying. Said she was pregnant. That it was mine."

"Oh, Dusty." I'm sure Ruby is drawing conclusions to why I freaked out about the condom.

"Farrah was distraught. She wanted to party, not be a mom. But I told her we'd figure it out. That I'd take care of her and the baby." My gut clenches over what was never meant to be. "I went to pick her up, but she had overdosed. She didn't make it."

"The baby?"

I shake my head. "I didn't love her anymore by then. I kept taking her back out of habit. But that baby. I coulda loved that baby."

Ruby crawls onto my lap and holds my face in her hands. "I'm so sorry that happened to you. I know you probably blame yourself, but it's not your fault. Some people can't live in this world right. They're too fragile inside or something."

There's something so earnest and pure about the way she's touching me. I didn't know I needed tenderness. I didn't know I needed someone to tell me it's okay that I couldn't save Farrah.

I didn't know I needed to need someone. But I do. I grasp one of her hands and kiss the inside of her wrist. "I'm supposed to be consoling you, I thought."

She smiles and my heart flies up in my throat.

When I kiss her, it's like our first kiss should have been. It's sweet and gentle.

It's just what I need.

Chapter Eight

Ruby

It seems to take forever for everyone to clear out of the main house and leave Dusty and me alone. But I'm nervous, so as much as I want them to go, I'm anxious and too restless.

I don't know what happens next. I feel like everything is too precious. I don't want to ruin it. But it feels like it's been so long since we made love. It hasn't, but so much has changed between us.

I'm too scared to put a label on it. But it's lovely and sweet.

He gets this "aw shucks" look on his face when he locks the front door behind the last of his crew. I think he's even blushing a little.

"So," he says.

"So," I repeat.

"I feel like I'm sixteen again. Not real sure what happens next."

I smile at his confession. "I have some ideas."

"Do you?"

"Want to hear them?"

"More than anything."

Crooking my finger at him seems to do the trick, and he crosses the room to where I am. I put his hands on my waist, and I loop my arms around his neck like we're at a middle school dance. It's both a little awkward and bittersweet. Like starting over before I knew what was before me. "Kiss me, Dusty. Like you did today. I want to feel that way again. Like the world is new again."

He starts at the tip of my nose of all places. Then he dots gentle kisses on my eyelids, my temples, my cheeks. When he finally, finally gets to my lips, he doesn't go for the hard slide. No, he's sweet and gentle. Soft glides, little nibbles. I sigh and part my lips to the gentle press of his tongue.

He steps back and turns me in the circle of his arms. I close my eyes, feeling the heat of his body behind me, the power of his grasp on me. "Ruby," he whispers in my ear. "What you do to me." His breath is warm against my neck, his body pressed up against mine so firmly. "Mmm," he purrs as his lips kiss my neck.

I push back against him, my soft curves meeting his hard, muscled body. He splays a hand against my abdomen and nibbles on my neck, the rasp of his day-old stubble stirring a wicked moan from me. He rubs circles on my stomach and a shiver wracks his body. Is he wondering if we made a baby yesterday? Does that make him hot?

A groan, more of a growl, rips from his throat, and he whips me around to face him.

"I need you." His mouth is on mine before I can respond, his arms pulling me tightly to his body. My arms slide up his chest, settling for a moment on his beating heart, then back around his neck to grasp him as firmly to me as he holds me.

I kiss him hungrily, my tongue twining with his. I clench the fabric of his shirt and my nails dig into the steel muscles beneath. He thrusts his body against mine, the hardness of his cock grinding into me.

I need to feel him. All of him.

My hands tremble at the buttons of his shirt until I can slide them across his skin, pushing the shirt off his shoulders. I rub my cheek against his chest hair and then test one of the flat disks against my tongue.

He grunts and clutches my head to him, so I suck that nipple into my mouth, reveling in the full-body shiver I induce. "Fuck, that's good."

I switch to the other side, my fingers tracing patterns over all his glorious skin. He's made to be savored.

Too soon, he pulls me off him. "I want to see you."

I want him to see me too.

I want to wow him. Own him. Tease him. Be owned by him, too.

I slowly, deliberately pulled the zipper down my dress. I turn, revealing my back and the exposed line of the red lace bra that I finally get to wear, knowing I put on that lingerie just for him. I can hear his heavy breaths as I push the dress down, revealing the red thong and my ass slowly, inch by inch. As the hem of the dress hits my ankles and pools around my feet, I coyly look over my shoulder to see him staring at me with his pants undone and that magnificent, heavy cock in his hand.

Oh wow. I'm stunned stupid by the sight.

"Them are some real pretty underthings you have on there, Miss Ruby."

I bite my lip and stare at his cock. "I hoped you'd like them, cowboy."

"Oh, I like them all right."

I'm practically panting when I reach around to unclasp my bra, but I hold it to my chest, still watching him stroke his hard cock. I turn further, showing him a bit more of those tits he loves so much, but just what isn't covered. I feel wanton and achy, and so very wet.

"Stay," he commands forcefully. "Right there."

His pants hit the floor and he steps out of them before striding across the room and scooping me up, my hands still holding my bra to my chest. He carries me to his bedroom and sets me down before sitting on the bed in front of me.

"Show me."

I let my hands go and my breasts spring free, warming under his gaze.

"You're the sexiest woman I've ever seen, Ruby."

I certainly feel sexy. Even though there's so much to learn about sex, I feel like a woman who knows secrets now. He reaches for me, but I lower to my knees and take in his surprised look.

My hands run over the top of his thighs, tantalizingly near his heavy balls. His breath hitches, but I glide my hands back down to his knees, pushing his legs apart as I go.

I settle myself comfortably between his knees and encourage his hips forward on the bed so that everything is within easy reach for me. Like a buffet of hot man.

I coo at him appreciatively, touching his granite shaft gently, enjoying the resulting twitch. "You're all mine now, cowboy." I cradle his large, heavy balls, weighing them in my hand, rolling them gently in my fingers before shifting my hands to the tops of his thighs again, and further up to his stomach, stroking through the whorls of dark hair there.

"Is this what you meant the other day when you wanted me to worship your cock?" I lean forward and lick him from root to tip, slowly, with the flat of my tongue. "Me on my knees. Tasting you. Needing you. Is this what you wanted?"

"Christ." It's a whispered groan, and he closes his eyes.

"That's what you meant though, right? Me, entranced with your cock. So far gone that I don't want to be anywhere but on my knees bringing it pleasure. So far gone that it is my whole world. My reason for taking my next breath. Is that what you want, Dusty?"

I slide my hands slowly back down to his legs, leaving my tongue in light contact with the tip of his cock as I do. "I'm going to enjoy this very much." I move away and place licks and kisses at the crease of his hip. I feel a little drunk, his earthy scent surrounding me. "God, you smell so good." I rub my cheek against his dick and am rewarded with another quiet groan.

I wrap both hands around his cock. "You're so thick. I love the way you stretch me when we fuck. I love your cock, Dusty. It's powerful, strong. Like you."

"Ruby, angel..."

My tongue flicks lightly over the tip of his cock and then swirls in widening circles. I use my tongue to trace down the underside of his shaft, turning my head sideways to lick and kiss the tender spot just where his cock meets his balls, lavishing him with attention. Showing him how important he is. I want to be his greatest fantasy.

I don't mind worshiping his cock. Not at all. It's about more than sex, even I know that. He needs it. He needs to know he's adored and honored. Accepted.

I'll be sad to go, but I'll always, always relish this connection we have.

Finally licking and kissing my way back up his dick, I grip him firmly near the base and work over the tip of his cock repeatedly, tasting the salty precum. I'm going on pure instinct. To pleasure him is to be pleasured.

My thong is soaked. I'm so turned on.

I look up to his face to find he is watching me with half-lidded eyes. I did that to him. Me. Smiling, keeping eye contact, I take him into my mouth until my lips meet my hand.

And I repeat. Over and over.

"Fuck, fuck, fuck." He's panting, groaning, moaning, and moving his hips as I increase the speed and pressure of my stroking.

All I want is his pleasure. It's my quest. To take as much of him into me as I can. To make him frenzied and out of control.

"You're going to make me come."

"Mmmm," is my answer, the vibrations on his dick causing him to gasp.

"Ruby, angel. Oh, fuck. You're a dirty angel, aren't you?" His voice is tight and strained. "You were made to suck my cock, weren't you?"

"Mmmm," I answer.

"You want to be my dirty, dirty girl? I'm going to come, Ruby. I'm going to come a lot. If you don't...fuck, fuck, fuck...I'm going to fill your mouth up if you don't..."

He pushes his hips up toward my mouth, thrusting frantically as his climax crashes over him and he roars. And I take it, the spurts coating my mouth and throat while he twitches. Time stops as he pulses in my mouth. It's salty and strange, but I like it.

I pull off and ease away as he flops onto his back. Completely spent.

"My God, woman. That was amazing."

My heart fills with pride. I know I'm a bit ridiculous, but I don't even care.

"C'mere," he commands, and I climb up onto the bed, resting my head on his chest.

"Nobody has ever made me feel like that before."

"I'm glad."

"When I get my strength back..."

"Oh, I know, cowboy. I'll be right here waiting."

We lay in silence, the setting sun shining shadows against the wall until it's almost completely dark except for the light from the living room. A few minutes later, I notice he's already hard. "Dusty?"

"I was just doing a mental replay." I chuckle, and he kisses the top of my head. "I feel so free with you, Ruby. Like I can say anything. Like you don't judge me."

"You can."

"I feel like I should tell you that sex isn't always like this. It can be great, but what we do, well, I've never felt anything like it before." I don't know what to say. I don't have experience, but I don't doubt him. I never in my wildest fantasies imagined sex would feel like this. "I like that I can say things to you, in bed, and be totally free and you know I still respect you."

I trace my hands through his chest hair. "I like that I can be a bad girl with you, but you don't shame me." His arms tighten around me. "It's like, I know you respect me, but we can just get down and dirty and it's safe."

"I really like being with you, angel."

"I like being with you too. I wish we had more time."

"I reckon we need to make the most of the time we have then." He rolls us over and covers me with all that strength. "Now I'm gonna eat that pretty little pussy of yours until you forget your name."

Dusty

SHE'S LEAVING TOMORROW.

I can't deal with it, so I try to put it in the back of my mind.

How the hell am I going to say goodbye to the best thing that ever happened to me?

I know from experience that you can't make someone want the same things you do. Hell, every time we have sex, I consider ripping off the condom, filling her up with my cum so I can put a baby in her and forcing her to stay. But I know that isn't how life works. She would wither and die here on the ranch if I took away her choices and bottled up her dreams.

And I can't say I'd do any better if I moved to Hollywood.

We're just too different.

But I fantasize that she's already pregnant. Every time I put my hand on her stomach, I'm hoping my child is in there. I'd love to watch her belly grow. I'd love to take care of her, protect her, keep her away from all those folks who want to use her up and throw her away. But Farrah taught me that you have to let people be free, even if it kills you inside.

And eventually kills them.

"What's got you in such a perky mood?" Carter asks as we muck out the stalls.

Hell, do I need to spill my guts to him? Are we living in some chick flick? I know women like to talk about feelings and such, but I can't see as how it can do any good. My experience, though, tells me that most women are smarter about things like that than we are.

Maybe it would be good to talk it out. I may as well give it a chance since I'm not exactly handling it very well on my own.

"Ruby leaves tomorrow."

"You catch feelings for her?"

"Yep."

"Sucks."

"Yep."

We go back to our chores. Is that it? That wasn't so bad. I feel like a real live Renaissance man. Next I'll be eating quiche.

Carter stops for water. "I knew about Marissa by our second date."

"Knew what about Marissa?"

He swallows some more. "That I was going to marry her."

I pause. "Did you tell her that?"

"Not on the second date, no. Didn't want to scare her off. But I knew. Sometimes you just know."

We work some more, and this time I pause for water. "How do you know?"

"It just kicks you in the ass, I guess. It's more than sex. It's like you can just breathe deep and you didn't realize you were breathing shallow all this time."

I cap my water. "It's sex too, though, right?"

Carter tips his hat. "Fuck, yeah."

I sit on a bale. "I thought it was love with Farrah. It ended up it wasn't."

"You two shared some powerful feelings. But not all of them were positive ones. She wanted your love, but she never knew what to do with it. You did the best you could with her, man."

"I always wonder if I did enough, though."

"There would never be enough for that girl. It wasn't your fault, what happened to her."

"Sometimes, I worry that she'd have been better off without me. That somehow I'm like a big black hole and that's why she died. What if I do that to someone else?"

Carter kicks my boot. "Don't be a jackass. It wasn't your fault."

I nod. Fair enough. "Not everyone is made for ranch living."

"You're building a fucking resort, Dusty. It's not like you're asking someone to join you in a pioneer lifestyle. And from what I hear, Ruby has been helping damn near everybody. She's got that computer set up for guests. She's been working with JT on a website. You told me she helped you pick out furniture for the cabins. Hell, I even saw her helping your uncle wash the limo yesterday. Seems like she fits in just fine here."

She hasn't gotten much reading done on her fancy Kindle, that's for sure. Ruby has some great ideas from working in hospitality. And she pitches in with everything. Farrah never would have learned how to use the lawnmower to help out.

"Sometimes, I think she's a fantasy I plucked out of the air. Like I took everything I ever wanted in a woman and made one up. Problem is, fantasies and reality are two different things. She wants to be an actress. And I can't give her the parties and the fancy cars. It's like Farrah all over again."

"You're an idiot. She's nothing like Farrah. How many times do we gotta have this conversation? You had a big old blind spot for that woman because you wanted to rescue her. But she didn't want to be rescued. Ruby ain't like that. She's strong. She can take care of herself and isn't going to drag you down. But if you are too chicken-shit to try then you don't deserve her anyway."

We go back to work. Maybe I am too chicken-shit. But I can't be the one to ask her to stay, to give up her dreams for me. If it's meant to be, she'll stay.

But I won't be the one to ask.

Chapter Nine

Ruby

As my plane touches down at LAX, a huge wave of guilt overtakes me.

I didn't say goodbye.

I sneaked away, telling Dusty we'd have lunch and he could drive me to the airport, and then when he was out on the back acres, I asked his uncle to give me a ride.

I just couldn't bear the thought of a goodbye. It was too painful. He's going to be mad, and he has every right to be, but I did what I had to do.

The last few days have been heaven on earth, but not once did we talk about feelings or futures or anything past the next day. I promised myself I wouldn't turn into a clingy mess. We had our vacation fling and now it's over.

I put my hand over my abdomen. Unless I brought home a souvenir.

I'm just sick thinking about what must be happening at Pair-a-Dice right now. Maybe nothing. Maybe he's secretly glad we didn't have the long goodbye with tears and promises we won't keep...or maybe he's hurt, sad, angry. I don't know. All I know is I somehow fell in love in just a few days and now my life seems even bleaker for it. Whoever said it was better to have loved and lost needs to pipe the fuck down. It sucks.

The Uber drops me off in front of my shitty apartment building. I want to run away. I don't belong here anymore. Maybe I never belonged in LA.

There's a padlock on my door. One I don't have a key to. I call Katie, but she doesn't pick up. I walk through the courtyard to the rental office. Deke is there. I hate Deke. Deke does the absolute minimum of work, and I count breathing on that list.

I start with a cheery smile, hoping maybe it will improve the tone of my voice. "Hey, Deke. Do you know why there is a padlock on my door?" I ask.

He yawns. "We were going to evict you, but Katie moved out. We haven't had a chance to change the locks yet, so we just put a padlock on."

I'm pretty sure that's illegal. I clench my jaw and then relax it into my cheery smile again. "Well, I actually still live there. I'm on the lease. I was just out of town. Katie didn't mention she was moving out."

A super long pause grows even longer. He yawns again. Scratches his belly. I want to leap over the counter and throttle him. "Katie said you moved. The apartment is empty."

My vision fills with red. "That can't be. All my stuff is in there. My furniture, my clothes, my laptop...everything I own."

"Nope. Empty. Saw it myself." He shrugs. I'm sure he's stoned. He's always stoned. "There was a box. I'll get it."

I'm still fuming when he comes back. Katie isn't answering her phone, of course. And why would she? She stole my stuff and now I have no place to live. He pushes the cardboard box to me. Inside, from what I can see, is all pictures. I take it and thank him. I'm not sure what else I'm supposed to do. I go back to my apartment, my old apartment, and just stare at the door. Then I sit on the curb.

Fine. I accept it. I'm defeated. It's over. I lost. Hollywood isn't for me.

I wonder what Dusty would say if I showed back up on the ranch. He's too nice to kick me out, but if he'd wanted me to stay, surely he would have at least hinted at it by now. No, that bridge is burned.

I don't have any choices left. My parents will take me in. There's nothing wrong with Ohio except that I wanted something else for a while. I don't want it anymore. The lying, the using, the struggling. All I ever wanted to do was act. So maybe I suck it up and do community playhouse productions and work behind the desk of a hotel and just...let this black hole go.

And get seven cats. And a membership to a wine club. I intend to drink a lot of wine in my new life as cat lady.

I stare at my phone, but can't dial the number. It's not pride. I don't have any of that left. What's stopping me? I try to run through my other options. Maybe work would give me a deal on a room for a few days. Maybe I could advertise for a roommate. One who already has an apartment would be best.

But I don't want to stay here. Not anymore. I want to be someplace where the pace is slower. Where people are friendlier. I don't mind hard work, but I'm tired of spinning my wheels. I want to accomplish something in a day and go to bed tired but satisfied with myself. My life.

I don't dare wish for what I want most.

Love. A family. A real home.

Dusty.

Really, that's what I want. I want the life I had the last few days. But that was a vacation. It was a step out of reality.

I don't think I'll ever find a man like Dusty again, and I certainly have no desire to go looking for one. Dusty is one of a kind. A real gentleman, a hardworking family man, and rough and dirty in bed. The whole package.

A shadow blocks the sun, and I realize someone has snuck up on me while I was wallowing. Stupid. I don't have my keys in between my fingers or my pepper spray out. I can't believe I was so careless. I've lived in this town too long to not be prepared for the worst.

I look up.

"Hello, angel. You forgot to say goodbye."

Dusty

I LOWER MYSELF TO THE curb next to Ruby, who seems in shock. "You sure surprised me today."

"Dusty, what are you doing here?"

She's a sight for sore eyes, for damn sure. I know I only just saw her this morning, but her absence from the ranch made time drag out for me. The fear that I'd done lost her. "Imagine what it was like to come back to the house and find you gone like a thief in the night."

"I'm no thief. I didn't take anything."

Anything except my heart.

"Why'd you run?"

"I wanted you to remember me in my white sundress and red lace. I was afraid I'd ruin everything by getting too emotional."

I'd have given anything to see some tears or at least regret this morning. I stretch my legs out in front of me and cross my ankles. "And getting emotional, that's a bad thing?"

"You signed up for a fling. What are you doing here?"

"Why are you sitting on the curb?"

"I asked you first."

Shit. I don't want to be brave. I want her to throw herself at me and tell me she loves me and doesn't want to leave me. That she wants nothing more but running a small resort on a ranch at my side. Why won't she break first?

"I'm here because I won't lose the best thing that ever happened to me without a fight." *Breathe, cowboy.* I take a deep breath. "I love you, Ruby. I can't give you a glamorous lifestyle and I'll never big sugar and own the kind of ranch that brings in the rich and elite, but you roped my heart that first day."

She hiccups a cry. "You love me?"

"I know you probably don't want to move to Pair-a-Dice, but maybe we can try a long-distance thing for now. Until you know one way or the other."

"You love me?"

"Woman, if you could just—"

I don't get the rest of the sentence out as my arms are filled with cotton candy sweetness and she's kissing my face.

"I didn't want to leave. I figured you didn't want me to stay."

"How'd you figure that?"

"Well, you didn't ask me to stay, for one thing."

"I didn't want to trap you or make you trade your dreams for mine."

"I love you, Dusty. I love you so much."

My cranky cowboy heart heats up. "Angel, you don't know how happy I am to hear that." I start kissing her and my body responds the way it always does. *Mine.* "Maybe we should take this inside. I don't reckon getting arrested for indecent exposure is a good way to start off our relationship."

"We can't go inside."

"Ruby, why are you sitting on the curb with all your luggage?"

"Yeah, about that..."

Chapter Ten

Dusty

Three months later

The full moon lights up the meadow and shines on the surface of the river. It's a perfect night. And my heart is lodged in my throat. I feel like a puddin' foot horse, unsure and awkward. But I don't want to be all hat and no cowboy—it's time I man up and make Ruby my wife.

"Dusty, this is beautiful. I can't believe you did all this."

I've set up overturned crates covered in white tea lights and those strings of battery-operated fairy lights in a circle around a little bistro table. "You've been working harder than anyone to get our grand opening ready. We're going to have a real nice season going into the holidays."

It was her idea to make the ranch a winter getaway too. We got it all set up for some holiday magic starting in a week. Reservations are filling up. We still have a lot to do, but we can accommodate guests while we do the rest of the upgrades. All thanks to Ruby and the way she has of taking my big ideas and finding ways to make them practical and doable. We're a damn fine team.

"This is all very romantic, cowboy."

"I was hoping you would think so." She's either going to make me the happiest man in the world, or I'm about to be chewing gravel. Either way, it's time.

I lead her to the table and pull out her chair, get her seated, and pour some of that wine she likes so much. It's not even fancy, though she deserves fancy. It's from a local winery, and she insists it's the best and I'm inclined to believe her.

And then I get down on one knee.

Her eyes get saucer big, and her fingers fly to her mouth.

"I want to make some promises to you, tonight." She nods, mute for a change. "I promise to love and take care of you for the rest of my life. I want to be the person you come to with your hopes and dreams, so I can help you achieve them the way you help me achieve mine.

"I never thought I could feel like this, and every time I think I love you as much as a man is capable, you open up another suite of rooms in my heart, so I can love you some more.

"I want you to be happy, that's the most important thing in the world. And if you're happy the way things are and you don't want to change them, I'll abide. But from this moment on, I want you to know that you're it for me. I want you forever, and I want to marry you. Tomorrow if you want, but if you want a big wedding then I'll abide that too."

Her pretty eyes are welling up with tears, and while I hope they're the happy kind, her tears still slay me. I pull out a ring, hoping to distract her some.

"Oh my God. Dusty!"

It's a pretty spectacular ring. "It was my momma's. Aunt Charlotte's been keeping it safe for me all these years. I didn't even know she had it until the day you flew back to LA." The pretty crinkle between her eyebrows means I'm not making sense. "Aunt Charlotte told me you'd gone and that before I decided what to do about it, I should take a look at the ring she'd been safekeeping for me to give to the woman I love someday. I knew when I saw it that it was only ever going on your hand and that I needed you to come back here."

"You've been thinking about it all this time?"

"I would have put it on your finger that day, but I didn't think you were ready. Especially after I found out you'd been evicted. I figured you needed to be sure you were here with me because you wanted to be and not that you didn't have any other choice. So I waited. And it's been killing me."

She slides to her knees so we're both on the ground. My girl never wants me to put her on a pedestal, she likes being at my side instead. "You are the love of my life, cowboy. You've shown me how to believe in something again, and every day you show me how to lead with kindness first and the rest will follow. I'm a better person because I met you. And I will marry you tomorrow, if you like."

My heart just busts open and I reach for her and pull her close. Too tight likely, but she's not complaining. "You just made me the happiest big ox on the planet."

"I'd like to make you happier."

I kiss her hair, the side of her face, her nose. "Not possible."

"I want to make a baby."

Ruby

I WANT DUSTY TO UNWRAP me like a present. All my senses are sharpened by my arousal. I can hear his heavy breathing and my own thundering heartbeat, and the quiet sounds of the forest as the soft breeze blows through the tall trees around us.

"Are you sure?"

Oh yeah. "I want your baby. I want to be pregnant."

"You know that turns me on more than anything. The thought of you. Fuck. Round and perfect. Everyone knowing you're mine."

I kiss him hard. The primal urge to mate so strong, stronger now that we're engaged. I start undoing his buttons.

"I brought condoms, angel. If you think we should wait..."

"I don't want to wait. I want to start forever tonight. Now."

"You're my fantasy. You know that, right? I can't wait to be inside you, nothing between us. I'm going to fill you up, angel." He undresses me, and his eyes explore my body, running over my breasts and down my stomach before settling between my thighs.

"Do you like what you see?" I ask, my face as innocent as I can manage, even though I don't feel very innocent at this moment. There's not a lot we haven't done, but this feels like a first time in some ways.

He nods. "Fuck, yes. You know I do."

Dusty undresses quickly but slows down when he sees the look in my eyes. He sends me an evil grin and slowly, too slowly, pulls the waistband of his briefs down his thighs, finally revealing his perfect, beautiful cock.

My mouth waters. My pussy clenches. I never get tired of looking at him. His shaft is thick and pink, and the head is engorged and already dripping. His balls are tight against his body, full and ready to give us a baby.

Oh my God. A baby.

Fascinated, I slowly reach out and run my finger across the tip of his cock, collecting the precum on my finger. His cock jumps when I touch it. I bring my finger to my mouth and suck, tasting him like it's the first time. "You taste good, Dusty." Like some powerful aphrodisiac.

"You taste better." He pulls my legs apart and crouches between them. He runs his tongue along my lips, then up to my clit over and over until my world explodes in light and color.

"Oh God, oh God, oh God!" I instinctively grab the back of his head to keep him close to me.

"That's right. Come for me. Get ready for my big cowboy cock."

Seconds later, he's inside me, thrusting with wild abandon, driving me to another orgasm. He holds onto my hips hard as he fucks me with more force until I am whimpering for another release. He's bottoming out, deeper than he's ever gone before. With every stroke, he throbs and my pussy tightens around him.

"Give me another."

"I can't."

"You fucking will."

I moan in response, and he grinds into me until I flood his cock, my juices saturating the blanket below us.

"I can feel you dripping down my balls, my dirty little angel. You're so hot for my cum, aren't you? You want it so bad."

I lose all control, calling out his name in ecstasy as wave after wave wracks my body with pleasure.

He cradles me against him, knowing that I'm most vulnerable after I come. "You want our baby, sweetheart? You want to be the mother of my child?" I'm so wrung out I can only nod in response. He growls and primal instinct takes over. Long deep strokes bring his cum flooding into me. I can feel it surging. He keeps thrusting, unable to stop until his cock goes soft.

He wraps his arms around me protectively, and I start to fall asleep, warm in his arms. He whispers his love for me as I begin dreaming about the baby I hope we just made.

Epilogue

Ruby

Five years later

"What's wrong with homeschooling?" Dusty asks me. "Your son needs to go to school with other kids. He's going to love it. You'll see."

My husband scowls at me. He's not ready to send our little guy off, and if I think about it too hard, neither am I.

"We could keep him home. We'll get that fancy homeschool curriculum. Hell, you're so smart, you can teach him all the math stuff."

"Are you going to finish painting that or should I call someone else?"

Dusty scowls at me some more and then turns his scowl toward the set he's working on. Opening night for the play at the community playhouse is in two weeks, but the director didn't like the mantel, so Dusty got volunteered to paint a new one.

I'm a tough director.

I've acted in a couple of productions over the years, but this is my first directing gig and I want it to be perfect. It never will be, but it feels good to have more control. I never even thought about directing when I lived in Hollywood. I was always so sure I wanted to be an actress. And I do enjoy acting still. Stage acting is much better than commercials. And directing has opened up a whole new passion for me.

"What happens if your water breaks on opening night?" Dusty asks. I think he's picking a fight.

"Well, we'll already be in town, so I guess that's a good thing. I figure I'll just head to the hospital after last curtain."

"Last curtain? The hell you will. Your water breaks and you tell me right away and we go directly to the hospital."

"You still have seven bricks left to paint."

"Ruby, promise me."

"I'm teasing you, Dusty." I put his free hand on my belly. "She's not due for a month."

He kisses my forehead. "Sorry I'm being such a bear. I get so damn nervous when you're pregnant. I just want to wrap you in cotton and feed you spaghetti."

"Oh now you're just being cruel." I've been craving spaghetti every day for the last four weeks. It doesn't matter if I eat it for breakfast, lunch, and dinner. I still want more.

"We should head back home soon. I want to check on the fence again."

Home. I love hearing him say *home*. It hasn't worn off yet. Not in the five years I've been living in Pair-a-Dice.

The resort is getting a little bigger every year. We've gotten more positive reviews than negative since the cabins were remodeled. And the saloon was built. Guests love having the saloon on the property, so they can have a few beers and not worry about cabs or cars.

This year, we've gone into weekly business. Instead of just booking for a few nights, we have a program that starts every Sunday. We're all-inclusive now, with planned activities and nightlife. Next year, we start a kid's program with counselors so parents can have some time to themselves during the day.

All in all, it's a lot to be proud of.

"Mommy! Daddy!" Dustin Jr. runs down the aisle, Charlotte not too far behind him, but the kid is fast.

Dusty scoops him up. "Hey, Junior. You have a good time at the grocery store with Aunt Charlotte?"

I wipe the chocolate off his face while he tells us all about the exciting cookie he got for "free, Momma, that means it don't cost nothin'" and that there is a new cereal that his Aunt won't get him, but we should know it will make him grow big and strong like his favorite superhero. He saw it on TV when he was visiting Uncle Carter.

It's all very exciting until I realize something is distracting me. A twinge. And then...

"Hey, Dusty, remember how we were talking about opening night and you made me promise to tell you if my water broke?"

"Yeah?"

"She hit her cue too early."

"Who did?" he asks, not understanding.

"Momma, why are you standing in a puddle?"

Also by Brill Harper

Blue Collar Bad Boys
Bounced
Nailed: A Blue Collar Bad Boys Book
Drilled: A Blue Collar Bad Boys Book
Wrecked: A Blue Collar Bad Boys Book
Laid: A Blue Collar Bad Boys Book
Tagged
Plowed
Bucked
Banged
Tapped: A Blue Collar Bad Boy Book

Dukes of Tempest
Mad Max
Dirty Dillon: A Small Town Age Gap Romance

Holiday Romance
The Demon's Curvy Angel: A Halloween Romance

It's Complicated
All Together
All at Once

Love in Brazen Bay
Wrong Number Text
The Right Stuff
So Wrong It's Right
Don't Get Me Wrong

Standalone
Dirty Jobs: a Blue Collar Bad Boys Collection
Notch on His Bedpost
Honeymoon With The Prince: A Royal Romance
Good Girl

Watch for more at https://brillharper.com.

About the Author

Unfailingly filthy...and super sweet

Brill's books are filthy/sweet for when you're in the mood for something a little over the top. Okay, a lot over the top. Sorry, not sorry. Members of the Brilliance Club get early access to all Brill's work and exclusive content not available anywhere else.

Find out more: **https://reamstories.com/brillharper**

Brill Harper is represented by Deidre Knight of The Knight Agency.

Read more at https://brillharper.com.

www.ingramcontent.com/pod-product-compliance
Lightning Source LLC
Chambersburg PA
CBHW031754150726
47989CB00006B/2716